Total-E-Bound Publishing books by Natalie Dae and Sam Crescent

Shades of Grey
Forced Assassin

I0570490

RUDE AWAKENING

NATALIE DAE and SAM CRESCENT

Rude Awakening
ISBN # 978-1-78184-552-3
©Copyright Natalie Dae and Sam Crescent 2012
Cover Art by Posh Gosh ©Copyright August 2012
Interior text design by Claire Siemaszkiewicz
Total-E-Bound Publishing

Published in 2012 by Total-E-Bound Publishing, Think Tank, Ruston Way, Lincoln, LN6 7FL, United Kingdom.

RUDE
AWAKENING

Prologue

Master clenched his teeth, furious at how she'd given him the slip. Margaret Savage—the common bitch he'd taken in, the woman he'd vowed to turn into a submissive lady—had gone out into the snow dressed inappropriately. He shouldn't be so surprised. Not a smudge of common sense in that head of hers, and why would there be? Why had he thought he could introduce any? She'd been brought up by a single parent on a run-down council housing estate. Hardly the kind of childhood where she'd know what was what. Not like women from his circles, those who were bred to do as they were told and understood how to behave. Still, Margaret was a fun adventure, part of a mission where he'd envisaged himself dragging her from rags to riches—riches she'd have to earn by being a good girl in the bedroom...something, along with learning common sense, she hadn't quite mastered.

Oh, he'd known this would be a frustrating task. Trying to change someone, change what was ingrained in them, wasn't as easy as his close fellow Master friends made it out to be. God, yes...you could teach submission to one who was willing to learn, but some of them happened to think they had a right in all matters, a right to speak up when something wasn't to their liking. It didn't help that there were men like Harry Knowles, who bleated about submissives needing to have their own voice — a safety net where they could stop play and basically gain control. What was the point in that? How could you be a Dominant yet allow your submissive to call the shots? It didn't make sense, went against everything he felt a D/s relationship should be. Submissives with a voice, indeed.

Uh, no. Not in his world.

Margaret had proved...stubborn right from the start. He'd chosen her because of her obvious need to be dominated. The way she'd lowered her head when he gave her an order in the library where she worked gave ample indication she longed for a hard Master. But he hadn't liked the confident air she'd had about her, strutting to the bookshelves to seek out the books he'd requested. That wasn't how he wanted any submissive of his to present herself. She'd needed a lashing, a good lesson in how to behave when around him. So he'd laid the groundwork, played at being the man of her dreams, and once she'd moved into his home, he'd changed the rules. He'd had to shut up her ever-questioning mouth and take her down a road she hadn't travelled before, one where punishments sat on every corner and stop lights — for him — didn't exist. He didn't stop when she asked him to, when she shouted or screamed out a safe word. No! What right did she have to expect that of him? To expect him to cease whipping just because she'd decided she didn't wish him to continue? She'd agreed to be his submissive, for goodness sake, and yet, when it came down to it, she quite clearly wanted to back out.

Silly little bitch.

After she'd lived with him for some time, he'd managed to make her solely reliant on him, changing her way of thinking a little so that she at least did as he asked, when he asked. She'd barely noticed the way he had done it—slowly, softly—and he'd congratulated himself on a sneaky job well done. But lately things had changed. She'd become strange, hard to read, and that hadn't sat well with him. Hadn't sat well at all.

This evening, as he'd ordered her to strip, she'd stared at him with defiance in her eyes. Oh, yes, she'd masked every other indication of insubordination very well, her body movements as they usually were, her mouth firmly shut against a tirade of questions she would undoubtedly have asked when they'd first got together, but those eyes...

Yes, they'd quite given her away.

How she'd escaped was a blur. One moment she'd been there, yielding under his fisted grip in her hair as he'd dragged her across the room towards the bed, and then the next she was gone, whippet-fast, long black hair flying behind her as she yanked open the bedroom door and fled down the stairs. Master had chuckled at that, knowing she would cower in the living room corner or try to squeeze into the kitchen larder in order to hide from him, hide from the beating she knew would follow.

He'd gone downstairs and searched the house for her, only to find she didn't occupy her usual spots. Found her winter boots still standing beside the front door as though a phantom wore them. Saw her coat still hanging on the hook beside his, her handbag next to it. The front door was slightly ajar — so slightly, he'd almost missed it but for the chilling breeze that snaked through the gap.

Hmm... Master had become angry then, striding to the front door and swinging it back, spotting her footprints in the deep snow. He'd told himself she would be back, that the biting cold on her bare feet would send her scurrying home, but after an hour had passed with still no sign of her, him pacing the foyer with a crop in hand ready to swipe it across her face the minute she returned, he realised she had more mettle than he'd given her credit for.

She would pay for that indiscretion.

And pay dearly.

Chapter One

Harry Knowles stood at the living room window of his large, secluded house, staring out into the darkness. Bored and feeling the huge need for a decent sub in his life, he gnawed at the inside of his cheek. The BDSM club wasn't producing the kind of sub he wanted lately — the women all insipid, inspiring nothing but tedium inside him. He wanted — *needed* — a challenge, a woman who had a unique brand of subservience, who knew how to do as she was told yet didn't obey without question. Someone who voiced queries, let him know what she wanted. Someone who employed a bit of dominance outside the bedroom — or dungeon — walls.

He wasn't holding his breath. After years of searching for the perfect partner, he'd failed to find one who even came close to matching his desires. The future didn't look very bright, and with a sigh, he resigned himself to a life of bedding women who weren't quite the ticket.

Winter had come on with a vengeance. Snow covered the grounds, his vast front lawn a blanket of white spotted with the odd indent from birds searching for worms in the cold, packed earth beneath. His gravelled driveway had been cleared when the first soft coat of snow had fallen in Manchester—his gardener, Len, had attached the snow scoop to the front of the Land Rover and shoved it to the sides. But since this afternoon, the drive had gained another thick layer of white, although two deep gouges marred the once-pristine expanse since Harry had driven over it as he'd arrived home from the office.

He sighed again, relieved it was Friday, that he wouldn't have to preside over his employees at his law firm until Monday. Yet the weekend stretched ahead, an interminably droll two days of him rattling around his house with nothing more to do than watch television or read thrillers.

His brother, David, lived in America close to their parents, so there was no chance of getting together with him and shooting the proverbial shit. Harry didn't mix business with pleasure, so employees coming over for dinner was out of the question, and the men who frequented the BDSM club... No, he didn't enjoy their company enough.

He didn't enjoy anyone's company much.

What the hell have I become? A successful businessman with no one to spend the money on or share my life with. Christ, this wasn't how I thought my life would be.

He clamped his lips together, annoyed with himself for walking down the road of self-pity. He had much to be grateful for, he knew that, yet a gaping hole sat in the middle of his life like an elephant in the room, taunting him every chance it got.

You're alone, Harry. Thirty-two years old and alone.

His thoughts turned to what he must appear like to other people. Stiff-backed, somewhat prickly, a man to be respected. A man who didn't let anyone in. His standards were perhaps a little too high in all areas. Maybe he needed to loosen up a bit, let his guard down a touch in order to get what he wanted. No woman found an uptight man attractive, no matter how appealing the packaging was. Oh, he'd heard whispers at the club from women he passed, who thought he hadn't heard their lurid remarks about his muscled physique and how they wished he'd whip them into shape. One woman had even gone so far as to mutter that burying her nose in the hair around his cock haunted her dreams.

Such things disturbed him, made him feel a prize to be won, a trinket dangling from a sub's arm— someone to be paraded as a good catch, looks, body, money and all. He prided himself on being able to spot a gold-digger a mile off, and perhaps that was his problem. He always suspected that was what they were after, so closed himself off, fucking them only with his cock and not his mind.

A slew of snow sailed down from above, startling him out of his pity party. He leapt back, feeling stupid, heart thumping at the sudden ferocity with which the snow had fallen. The roof was clearly overburdened. He moved closer to the window, peering out and seeing a stack of snow that almost reached the outside windowsill. If the weather kept up like this, Len would have his work cut out for him come Monday morning.

Harry turned from the window and stared around his living room, the opulence nothing but just the contents of his home to him. To others it would appear the height of elegance, all dark red walls and rugs, two deep-seated leather sofas in cherry hide, their backs studded with buttons, sitting opposite one another, a highly polished walnut coffee table in between. A real fire crackled in the grate, the fireplace a huge monstrosity he'd had installed with the image in mind of him and that special woman in his life sprawled on the rug in front of it—touching, caressing, exploring.

How was it he'd attained every other dream except that one? Was he being greedy in wanting the icing on the cake—a woman to love and adore, to share his wealth and life with?

It seemed he was.

He huffed out another sigh and turned his back on the room, returning to the window. Trees as tall as ten men bordered the edge of his property, so far in the distance they appeared merely bushes. The clouds, heavily pregnant with snow, made the sky appear a mid-grey instead of the true night-time blackness they shrouded. Moonlight somehow filtered through them, though, touching the grounds with fingers of silver, bouncing off the whiteness covering it. A few specks of snow danced, as though afterthoughts to the deluge that had teemed down not an hour since, and he prayed no more would fall tonight.

Something white ghosted out of the trees, a wisp of movement that darted for a moment then disappeared. Another chunk of snow falling from the branches, perhaps, or a figment of Harry's imagination. A chill sped up his spine and he shivered, wondering why he felt so cold when the fire blazed. Staring at snow would do that. Despite being enveloped in warmth, when looking out at the scene before him, he knew full well how to imagine being frozen out there. The chill dispersed, and he shrugged, spinning on one heel in search of where he'd placed his brandy earlier. He spied the cut-crystal glass on the walnut sideboard beside the door, a few mouthfuls of liquid still inside—liquid that would ensure the chill was kept at bay.

He strode over and picked up the glass, downing the brandy in one gulp, pleased at the fiery burn that spread through him. He poured another and took it to the window, cursing himself for the torture he was inflicting by idling away his evening like this. Boredom—it filled every fibre of him, taking a firm grip and not letting go.

Mind over matter. He knew all about that and pushed himself to think of something interesting to waste away the time. He could go out to the club, select a woman and book a dungeon for a few hours, losing himself in sex and control.

But it doesn't work out like that, does it? I want more. Something… Christ, just something more.

He stared at the tree line, and damn, there it was again, that flick of white. Were there red squirrels in the treetops, scurrying across the branches, dislodging snow? Instead of disappearing, the smudge of movement increased, darting left to right, growing arms that spread out to the sides.

Was that a damn person out there?

Harry pressed his nose to the glass, annoyed when his heated breath misted the pane and obscured his view. He stepped to the side and looked out again. Yes, someone was out there, he was sure of it. Stomach knotting, the chill returning, he tossed the brandy down his throat then glanced at the trees again. The shape was still there, larger now, as if whoever was out in such foul weather was making for his house. He left the window and placed a guard in front of the fire, then picked up his mobile and slipped it into his trouser pocket.

Out in his large foyer, he opened the built-in coat cupboard and took a sturdy pair of boots from the shelf, pulling them on and tucking his trouser hems inside. He selected a heavy black coat — fine wool that kept out the cold when he turned up the collar — then wound a grey scarf about his neck. He slipped his hands into black leather gloves and, on instinct, grabbed another of his coats from a hanger and draped it over his arm.

He closed the cupboard door and took his keys from a hook beside it, putting them in his coat pocket. He went back into the living room to look out of the window, and although the shape had gone, he decided to go outside and check anyway. That smudge had grown arms, he was sure of it, and even if it turned out to be his imagination, he couldn't live with himself if...

He left his house, a blustery, spiteful wind shunting him back a step, as though trying to prevent him investigating. The strength of the cold was an utter shock to his system, and he shoved his hands into his coat pockets and took a lung-freezing breath to steady the tingle of nerves swirling in his belly.

Harry trudged through the snow towards where he'd last seen the shape. It was a way ahead — damn him for having such a big front lawn! — and he kept his gaze on the spot, snow gripping his boots in what he felt was an attempt to stop him walking.

What were those fanciful thoughts all about? Wind and snow didn't have minds of their own, and he'd be damned if he was going to allow his idle brain to conjure scenarios that couldn't possibly exist. He pushed on, determined to reach his destination, his stubbornness lending him the strength his legs needed to wade through the snow.

He was almost there so took his hands from his pockets and shook out the spare coat, dashing away the stray flecks that had attached to the material. He peered ahead at a large indent, the inside walls of it about forty centimetres high. Beyond it was a channel gouged into the snow, a wavy line where someone had struggled to walk from the tree line. His heart stuttered, banged against his ribs so hard the bones felt tender, and he released a ragged breath that puffed out as a white cloud.

As he neared the edge of the indent, he stared down to see a woman lying on her side, her hands closest to him, arms stretched above her as if she'd reached out to the house. Her long, black hair fanned out in snow-clumped hanks, and he'd swear the ends were frozen. All that covered her was a denim mini-skirt and a red V-neck sweater. A collar surrounded her neck, cheap black leather, and it appeared to be too tight, the skin around it chafed. Legs, bent at the knees, were red raw, the woman having possibly crawled a short way, or even all the way from the trees. And no shoes on her dainty feet either. Shock and surprise rendered him unmoveable for a moment, even though his mind screamed that he reach for his phone and call for help.

"Jesus Christ!"

He dropped the spare coat—a violent splash of crimson—and went down on his knees, tucking his hands beneath her and dragging her towards him. With her torso draped across his thighs, he cradled her head in one arm and snatched the glove off his free hand with his teeth. Hand trembling, he touched two fingers to her neck...which bore what he recognised as a collar. He was relieved to find a faint pulse—but it was extremely faint, and if she stayed out here much longer it would fade completely. With some difficulty, due to her floppy body and his arms seizing up from the cold, he managed to wrap her in the coat, conscious of the blue tinge growing rapidly around her plump mouth. He laid her on the ground then stood, scooping her into his arms. He estimated her weight at not much more than one hundred pounds, and the brief thought entered his head as to how she had become so thin or whether she'd always been that way.

Holding her close, he staggered back the way he had come, using the path he'd created. His house seemed too far, mocking him from the distance, and he upped his pace, clenching his teeth against the throb of his protesting thigh muscles. At last he reached home, and, lifting one knee so he could balance her back across it, he managed to push open the door without dropping her.

Inside, heat smacked him with as much ferocity as the wind had when he'd first come out, and he slammed the door shut with his boot sole. Quickly, he moved into the living room, placing her on the deep-pile rug before the fire, wondering if that was the right thing to do. So much heat after so much cold might make her ill. Whatever—he followed his instincts and removed the coat and her clothes, tossing them aside. He laid her out on her back and checked her pulse again—still faint but there—and massaged her limbs for what seemed a great length of time. He noted he still wore one glove but dismissed the thought. It didn't matter, so long as he brought warmth to her body.

Would she wake? Should he call an ambulance? How long would it take for one to arrive in this weather? His house was out in the sticks, the roads virtually impassable. He'd been lucky to get home tonight, his car slewing all over the road, snide ice lurking beneath the snow. So long as she was alive, he determined it would be okay to continue what he was doing.

The snow in her hair melted, leaving dark patches on the rug. Her lips gradually lost their blueness, a rosy pink replacing the previously frightening colour, and her cheek closest to the fire took on the red of warmth, not the raw scarlet of cold.

Her eyelids flickered, and he sucked in a sharp breath when they opened fully and bright blue eyes stared back at him. He breathed out, so pleased to see her awake, and smiled to give her reassurance.

"I found you outside," he said, feeling stupid in stating the obvious.

She struggled to get up, eyes growing wider, darting from side to side in panic.

"It's all right, I won't hurt you," he said, unsure what the hell to say to take that scared, pained look from her face. "What were you doing outside? Is there someone I can call? Family, so they can come and collect you?"

She shook her head, leaning back on her elbows, ribcage prominent like a fishing creel covered in skin. He gritted his teeth at the lengths some women went to for what they thought was the perfect figure, when, in fact, he suspected bones dressed in a thin layer of flesh didn't truly appeal to any man.

"A hot drink," he said, standing and holding his hand out. "And a blanket?"

She nodded again, and he took her hand, tentative to do so at first in case he scared her. But she took it, pitifully bony fingers curling around his, and he led her from the living room and out into the foyer.

"I have blankets in here," he said, jerking his head at the coat cupboard. He opened the door and reached inside to a shelf, tugging a blanket free and handing it to her.

She let go of his hand and accepted the tartan fleece, wrapping it about her shoulders quickly, as though finally recognising her naked state. Her whole body shook, her teeth chattered, and her eyes appeared large in her tiny, pixie-chinned face. Where on earth had she come from? What life had she led that made her look half-starved and frightened? And what the hell was she doing outside in a snowstorm?

Those questions and more fizzed on his tongue, but he refrained from asking them just yet. Bombarding her too soon might see her taking flight again, and until he could hand her over to someone who cared for her, he'd keep his probing to a minimum.

"Come this way," he said, cursing himself for sounding the toff people thought him to be. "To the kitchen."

He walked across the foyer to a door beside that of the living room and pushed inside. He flicked on the light and held the door open for her, guiding her across the room, as she shivered on shaking legs, to one of the pine chairs around the matching table.

"So there is no one I can call?" he asked again, gently, pouring still-hot coffee from his percolator and adding four spoons of sugar in case she was in shock. He'd heard sugar was good for that. Whether it was true or not remained to be seen.

"No," she whispered, accepting the mug in both hands, taking a healthy gulp and wincing.

"I see." He pulled out a chair opposite and sat, watching her for signs of distress. "Your name then?"

"I...I don't remember."

She took another sip, her body shaking less, though it still gave a violent jerk now and then.

"You don't remember?"

As she shook her head and turned away from him to stare at his back door, he wondered if she was getting ready to bolt. If she did, there wasn't much he could do about it, short of holding her prisoner while he called the police then let them deal with her.

"Hmm," he said, his need to fill the silence strong. "Do you know why you were outside with no coat on?"

"No," she said, sipping, still staring outside.

"Are you happy to stay here until the morning? Until we can figure out what to do? I doubt an ambulance or the police—"

"No!" she said, snapping her head to face him. "Don't call anyone. No one at all. I'll be all right. If I can just stay here until...until I know who I am, then I can go back home."

How long would that take? He wasn't versed in the medical field, but he knew amnesia could sometimes last years. At some point she would have to leave, he'd have to let the authorities take care of her, but despite her having no apparent recollection of who she was, he skated on thin ice with regards to keeping her here. As a lawyer, he knew if she was aware of who she was, she might not want to stay here at all, and if he allowed her to stay when she wasn't sure of her own mind, he could be in a heap of trouble.

Monday. She can stay until Monday.

"All right," he said, scraping his chair back and wincing at the harsh sound it made on the slate floor tiles. "We'll leave it over the weekend, but only on the condition that as soon as you remember who you are, you must tell me. People could be worried about you." He decided to push it a little more. "And considering your...appearance, it doesn't look like you've been eating too well recently."

She let a small smile touch her lips and drank more coffee, gaze straying back to the door.

"Do you want to leave?" he asked, giving her the option despite his instincts shouting that she couldn't walk back out there tonight.

"No," she said. "No."

"Are you looking at the door for any specific reason?"

"Yes. Wondering if it's locked."

"Yes, it's locked. It's night-time and I live in the middle of nowhere, so it needs to be lock —"

"Good." She nodded. "Good."

She relaxed, her shoulders slumping, and Harry wondered what the bloody hell had happened to make her so skittish, so obviously afraid of something.

"I'll need to call you something while you're here," he said.

"Anything. Call me anything you like." Her voice was so thin, so...quiet.

He regarded her for a moment, seeing her as he'd found her — asleep in the snow, her mouth blue, legs so red.

"Ruby," he said. "That all right?"

"Yes," she said, her smile growing a little wider. "That'll do just fine."

Chapter Two

What the fuck have I just done?

Ruby — she liked the sound of that — closed her eyes and sipped her coffee, loving the hot liquid rushing down her throat. Running out in the snow had been a really fucking stupid idea, but at a time like that, the weather hadn't been on her mind. Not only had it been bloody stupid, now she was trapped with another man and there was no way on this earth she was going back outside and freezing her tits off. It was not happening, not today.

"Once you've finished your coffee, I'll show you to the spare room, then you can take a bath. I'll get your clothes laundered."

The hot guy in front of her kept trying to reassure her, but no matter how strong she tried to be, her attention kept straying to the kitchen door, with her expecting to see him.

She touched the collar at her neck and a shiver ran through her body. What would happen if he found her? No, she couldn't think like that. Against all odds, she was free…and intended to stay that way.

"What's your name?" she asked.

The man who'd taken her in stood and moved out of her space but within distance — she suspected in case she suffered with any after-effects of the cold. A really sweet gesture, and one Ruby would keep in her heart always.

Ruby. It was a rather fitting name and one she was going to keep for a while. Her real name, Margaret Savage, left a lot to be desired. A horrible thing to have lied about her memory, but the less he thought she knew about herself, the less it was likely he'd go running to the police. Keeping a low profile was all that mattered at the moment.

"Harry." His voice was direct and left no room for argument every time he spoke.

Ruby sipped from her cup and took the time to look at him.

Harry, her protector, was a tall and striking man. 'Built like a brick shit house', her mum would say, but to her, Harry was sex on legs. Top notch, the dog's bollocks.

He stared down at her as if commanding her to his will, and from years of abuse — sorry, training — she averted her eyes and drank the rest of her coffee. The liquid burnt another welcome path. Although his gaze didn't unnerve her like his had, she needed to get away from this stranger and have a shower. Touching the collar again from months of habit, she waited for the usual commands of her body. Then, realising her Master was no longer with her, Ruby lifted her head and smiled at the man before her.

No longer a dog to be kept and ordered around, she was free to live her life.

Unless he found her.

"Do you have a last name?" she asked.

"Not one I'm willing to divulge at the moment, no."

His voice, for some unknown reason, made her feel protected. And wow, was he ever posh. He must be one of those toffs working in a high-end job. With a house like this, and the obviously well-cut clothes he wore, he inhabited a world she'd only ever seen on TV. The type of person who looked down on the likes of her, unless they wanted a bit of rough with a common girl from a council estate.

Ruby cursed her life and her upbringing. A standard education, and brought up in an area considered 'rough', Ruby believed she'd made a decent way in her life despite the pitfalls. Long before meeting the bastard, devil incarnate, that was. A library assistant didn't pay very well, but she loved her job. Though, the library had been the place the bastard had found her.

More than five years had passed since he'd come into the library, wooed her and taken her away from her life. No more second-rate flats or dead-end boyfriends. No, she'd fallen in love with who she'd thought was a decent man. Then it had turned out he wasn't so decent, and her life had turned to shit.

Another thing—she really needed to stop swearing.

"I'm ready for the bath or a shower," she said.

He nodded. She smiled and followed him out of the kitchen, clutching the soft blanket around her. How she managed to contain her gasp of surprise was beyond her. The house was more like a mansion.

"Do you actually live here?" she asked. "You know, own this gaff?"

Harry turned abruptly and gave her a funny look.

"I was only asking." Jesus, what got his goat?

She looked away from him and gazed at the walls in the hallway — a hallway bigger than her mum's living room. How the other half lived! The paintings alone must have cost more than she'd made in a year. They were so beautiful — classic art she reckoned. She'd seen some in books and wasn't sure if she believed they were the real deal — artwork of the universe and interpretations of still life so breathtaking that she fell behind to look closer.

She was brought out of her awe when he cleared his throat — in a very uptight kind of way — and tapped his foot.

Strange man.

"I'm so sorry. Your artwork is amazing." She pointed behind her and wondered why the hell she was trying to show him when it was obvious where his bloody art was.

He simply moved on towards the uncarpeted stairs, some kind of polished dark wood that shone from the light of a chandelier.

What the fuck's his deal?

Instead of over-thinking his rejection and obvious dislike of her, she took the time to admire his arse.

How long had it been since she last appreciated an arse where Master wasn't present to yell at or ridicule her?

Too long.

Harry's was tight, hard, and for a split second she imagined sinking her fingers into the flesh, holding him closer to fuck her harder. The image, shocking and sudden, shook her to the core. No man had made her feel that way. Those times and images were long gone, banished by the greater fear of the whip or far harsher punishments. Whips brandished not to give her pleasure-pain but to hurt, to make her know her place. On the surface, to anyone who might have been watching, the whippings looked like any other normal play, but when his temper had been really rife and she'd been unable to scream or break free, she'd suffered unimaginable pain. Oh, she didn't need to imagine the pain now—she knew first-hand how a badly wielded crop could make you want to die rather than feel another strike. Some scars were still present on her back, faded as they all became with time, but still there.

The scars inside her heart and mind, though, they were another matter.

She trailed Harry up the stairs.

Times when she thought about her past—because it was her past now, and her present was here for however long Harry let her stay—she wondered why Master had picked her. Out of so many other women—other women who'd gladly do as they were told with no second guesses—he'd chosen her, someone who had spoken up when she wasn't supposed to, who questioned him.

He'd soon beaten that out of her.

Her life, her very upbringing, had hindered any positive relationship she could've had with him. Growing up on a council estate where you got bullied for being different made her, as a child, steer away from making many friends. She didn't go out much, and when Master had come into the library, with his kind words and soft gestures, she'd thought she'd found her equal, someone who enjoyed a woman who wanted to learn, wanted to understand every aspect of BDSM.

She soon found out it wasn't her job to learn. Not the kind of lessons she'd had in mind, anyway. Her job was to learn a totally different lesson—do as you're fucking told. After a time, she'd realised he manipulated things so she was in the wrong and he had an excuse to punish her.

Fuck, don't cry now. Keep it all together.

At the top of the stairs, Ruby followed Harry down a long corridor filled with several doors.

"Well, is this your house?" she asked again.

Please tell me I haven't just stumbled upon one of the richest men alive. Tell me you're looking after this place. I so don't need my life to go to shit like that, getting involved with another damn toff.

He stopped suddenly and she collided with his back. Her gasp and inhale brought a giant whiff of his wonderful, natural scent. Harry Something-or-Other had it going on in all departments.

"Sorry," she mumbled, stepping away from him.

Crap. A blush was spreading to her cheeks. She tried to cover it with some of her hair, but he reached his hands out and stopped her.

"Don't shield any of yourself from me," he said gently.

Her vocal cords went into retreat, and she stood still as he pushed her hair off her face, his fingers brushing across the sides and back of her neck. Goosebumps erupted on her skin and she gasped, the tightness in her muscles doubling against the onset of arousal — arousal so quick and unexpected Ruby couldn't account for it. Not daring to look up, she kept her gaze firmly on his hard chest. A wide, protective chest, one that would surround her as he made love to her.

Where were these erotic thoughts coming from? Master only evoked fear and loathing. This — the thick pulse of warmth between her legs and the tingling sensitivity on her arms and body — could only be described as the instant arousal she'd experienced too long ago to remember.

Her solace to the situation with Master had been to bring herself to orgasm. Had she ever reached orgasm with him? She did once or twice, and was truly amazed at her inability to recall all the amazing sensations lovemaking could bring to a woman—until now. Even when pleasuring a man, she'd found some form of happiness in the act.

"Of course I own this house. What did you think? I was some stray off the street?"

His words struck a chord with her. She was a stray off the street. Biting her lip, she kept her eyes downcast, her usual defence against seeing derision and repulsion in someone's eyes.

"You never know, stranger things have happened at sea," she muttered.

"We're not at sea and the reference is completely irrelevant."

Oh, God. He thought she was stupid. He sounded like some sort of teacher with the way he spoke. Sure, she'd read plenty of books in her time, was well learned even if she did speak coarse and common, but come on—'the reference is completely irrelevant'? Was that kind of response really necessary? It was a figure of speech, not something that needed argument.

"I apologise. I'll keep my silly statements to myself," she said, cheeks blazing hotter.

He turned away and Ruby couldn't resist sticking her tongue out at his back.

"That act simply makes you immature and makes me feel the need to call child services."

Ruby jumped, looking all over his back for some kind of third eye.

How the fuck did he see that?

"I see from your shock you're wondering how I saw you pulling the predictable face of sticking the tongue out. Well, from your attitude it was easy to predict, but then it helped having the aid of a mirror there."

Harry pointed to the wall opposite and there it was. She had been so struck with her thoughts and his fine arse she'd failed to see the mirrors dotting the spaces between doors along the entirety of the landing.

Had he seen her checking out his arse? She hoped not. Embarrassed, she looked down at the floor and prayed for it to open up and take her, to end the torment.

She expected to stop outside one of the many doors, but eventually they went up another flight of stairs, where there were more doors and mirrors.

Ruby couldn't contain herself any longer. It seemed being free of Master had loosened her tongue. "Why do you have lots of mirrors?"

He stopped at one of the doors, which looked like so many others she'd passed. He opened it and invited her to move in before him.

The room was so typically a rich-man guest room. A four-poster bed dominated the space, a wardrobe and a few other pieces of mahogany furniture butted against the walls.

"This is one hell of a room," she pointed out, and for the first time she heard him chuckle and saw him grin.

The sound was so different from his previously gruff manner. They'd known each other no longer than thirty minutes and already she'd detected that he very rarely smiled. Such a shame—his was so charismatic. She wanted him to keep it firmly in place as it touched a piece of her heart—a piece unused to being warmed by such a small thing.

"It's quite refreshing having a woman here who's not used to all these amenities."

Amenities?

"You're aware we're in a mansion and not a campsite, right?" she asked. "I mean, I'm sure you have a loo somewhere along here. The amenities can't be very far away." She ploughed on, her tongue even looser now. "And me being the kind of woman who isn't used to those amenities... Please, just say I'm common and be done with it."

She stared at him, saw the shock and surprise on his face, then looked at the floor, a gesture ingrained in her, even if she had found her voice again. She thought of camping to take her mind off his hot stare at the top of her head. She loved camping, and thinking about it brought on a smile. Nothing like being outside and fending for yourself, the entire experience bringing you closer to the joys of nature. Not right now in the snow and sub-zero temperatures, but during spring and summer months the prospect always appealed.

His scoff broke through her happy, holiday thoughts. "I wouldn't dream of camping. Hotels all the way."

Of all the people to rescue her, Ruby was stuck with a man who was uptight and didn't like camping like the little people.

She didn't know if she would have been in better company with the mounds of snow outside.

"I'm sorry you think that. You've obviously had really bad camping experiences." Ruby shrugged, not knowing what else to say. From the few words they'd spoken, it was clear they were worlds apart.

"Why do you keep fingering that collar?" he asked, suddenly coming closer.

Ruby instinctively took a step back and covered the band of ownership with her hand. She wasn't allowed to let anyone touch it. She didn't even know how to take it off. She'd spent so many times almost strangling herself by yanking it. It was tight as hell.

She refused to tell him. "Where is this bath?"

He walked forwards, and it brought a lump to her throat as she backed up against the wall. She'd tried to distract him away from that question, but it was obvious he was adamant in hearing her answer.

"Don't be afraid." He held out a hand. "I won't hurt you, but I want to know why you keep touching that. How you got it."

Despite his gruff ways, Ruby wasn't afraid of him. He may have the presence of a giant, but like giants before him, he seemed as though he would be tame unless fought with. No, it was the fear of what he'd do to her that scared her. The beating she'd once taken when removing another simple black collar had drilled it into her early on—she was to keep it on and nothing this man said would make her remove it until she was ready and sure of her safety.

The collar would stay for now—Master's last bit of power over her, but the fear of him finding her without it was indescribable.

"Please show me where the bathtub is." She cringed at the shaking in her voice, her body a quivering mess of nerves.

Holding her breath, she watched him remove her hands from the band. Her skin beneath was sore from her constant rubbing. He touched the collar and frowned. Ruby didn't know what to say or what to do, so she kept holding her breath until she saw stars.

He touched her stomach and asked her very gently to breathe. Harry assisted her while she came down from her terror, and she released her breath in one long, slow exhalation.

"Someone hurt you badly," he said.

She remembered her situation—that he thought she'd lost her memory. She could use the lie from earlier to help her now. "I don't know." With all of her might, she wished she really didn't know.

"Keep your secrets for now." Harry opened the door to her left. "There is your bathroom. Towels, toiletries—everything you'll need to get clean and feel like a woman is in there."

Ruby nodded and moved past him. She wrapped the blanket closer around her, trying to create a layer of insulation to stop her showing how terrified she really was.

"I'll get some of my old clothes for you to wear. I won't have anything for a lady, though."

Ruby noted the word lady used instead of woman. Who was this man? Had he stepped out of some old-fashioned movie?

She was so out of place in the whole house.

When Ruby was sure he'd left, she went into the bathroom and closed the door. She sighed in exasperation. There was no lock.

Resting her head against the wood, she closed her eyes for a moment then opened them as she turned to look at the room. More mirrors. The guy—Harry—was obsessed with them. She didn't want to look at herself. She no longer wished to see the pitiful excuse of a woman she'd turned into. After all of her mother's work to make her independent and hard-working, to fight for her right to an opinion and everything else her mother thought she needed in her adult life, here she was. At the mercy of a man she didn't know, surrounded by the most beautiful artwork ever seen, and running from a Master who thought he could use her in the most callous of ways. No getting away from it. Her mother would be embarrassed.

Shaking her head of the awful negativity claiming her, filling her, Ruby walked to the tub which stood in the centre of the room like a glorious statue. It looked as though it could hold three people easily, twice the size of a normal bath and God knew how much it had cost...and this was just a guest room?

The more she thought about her surroundings, the more uncomfortable she became. Before her life had turned to shit, she'd rented a simple little flat...no, apartment. A one-bedroom, second-floor apartment in an up-and-coming area—a far cry from the place where she'd been brought up. Once he had entered the equation, the freedom and the apartment went, along with her job at the local library. The more time she dwelled on the changes in her life back then, she saw a new aspect and level to the changes. He'd made her completely, one-hundred per cent dependant on him, and now she was fleeing like some criminal instead of the victim she'd become.

Ruby pushed the plug into the hole and ran the water, testing the heat. She found some salts and soap and placed them around the edge for easy reach. The salts were lavender and the scent made her drowsy. Pulling off the blanket, she climbed into the hot water and allowed herself the luxury to relax. Bath time had become a chore where Master inflicted other untold evils on her body, and it was nice to be left to lie back and enjoy the scents.

You did it, Ruby. You got away and you no longer have to worry.

The name Ruby stuck more than her birth name, and she liked it. A fitting name for her new life. Placing a hand to the collar—it seemed to be an action she couldn't stop—she wondered how long it would be before she removed it. The collar was a symbol of possession and an honour not only for the submissive to wear but an honour for her Dominant in the fact she'd chosen him to be her protector and Master. But the collar around her neck was ownership and had a different meaning intended than the development of increased feelings.

Don't think about him. Don't give him the power he's taken from you for so long.

A tear slid down her cheek, and for the first time since the start of her life with Master, Ruby allowed the tears to fall without fear of being caught. First one and then two, and with time they increased, a silent, wet protest against the agony she'd somehow survived. No noise escaped her, and Ruby was thankful, proud of herself for mastering how to cry unheard. Tears had meaning to them, but talking to Harry about her tears would highlight that she knew who she was. He was still a stranger, and knowing her luck he might know Master and would be obliged to give her back.

She wiped the tears from her eyes and stared at her bitter reflection in a mirror opposite.

"This is it, Ruby. The last time you'll ever allow that bastard to control you. Your tears and fears must end now," she whispered, hoping deep in her heart that she would one day look in the mirror and see the fun and vibrant woman she'd once been. A small part of her had come back with her responses to Harry, so there was hope, wasn't there?

She took a sponge and lathered it with the heady-smelling soap. Did Harry use the same? The man had sure smelt fantastic, like the best soap ever.

Clearing her thoughts of the threat of Master, Ruby used the time to herself to soap her body and hope the cleansing of the dirt brought about the cleansing in her heart and soul.

The collar itched, and she hoped one day she'd have the courage to remove it.

It stood out, ugly and disgusting against her pale skin. She sank down beneath the bubbles to hide it. She loved being underwater, the silence amazing buffered from the natural sounds of the outside world.

One day, she promised herself. One day she'd be back to who she was. Happy, fighting for life, and with a man who loved her and wanted her love.

Ruby smiled, coming up for air.

She could live and hope for her dream to come true.

Chapter Three

Harry took the two flights of stairs back down to the living room, shutting out images of Ruby in the bath. The last thing he needed was to allow her to snake inside his heart, to allow feelings for her to develop. He would get through this weekend, and if she hadn't regained her memory by Monday morning, then she would have to go.

He scooped up her wet clothing and went to the kitchen, entering the laundry room through a door beside his red double oven. He placed her garments in the washing machine, adding detergent and switching it on while he entertained thoughts of her collar. She was quite clearly a submissive and belonged to someone, had perhaps run from that person, judging by her lack of footwear and coat. Maybe her mind had shut down when she'd passed out from the cold, but he wanted answers and didn't quite believe she'd lost her memory.

No matter. He'd coax information out of her.

There was something about her that hadn't seemed right to him, her words somewhat coarse yet laced with proper speech, as though she'd affected her accent to fit in with him. He'd encountered people like that before, who adopted a refined way of speaking so he thought they were from his class. He frowned, annoyed that people felt the need to do that. Why not just be themselves? Did they think him so shallow he wouldn't accept them?

Ruby's neck was sore around her collar, and her constant lifting her hand to it, worrying the leather, told him she did this gesture often and without realising. It was too tight, and he'd noticed there was no buckle but a small keyhole in the back. Removing it would require it being cut off.

He returned to the kitchen and switched the kettle on. As it boiled, he selected a few cold cuts from the fridge, a wedge of quiche and some pickles, and buttered some slices of French bread. Anyone in their right mind could see she didn't eat much, and as he hadn't found out how long she'd been outside, he could only guess that she must be hungry.

She shuffled into his peripheral vision then, once more wrapped in the tartan blanket, only this time she'd secured it beneath her armpits. A towel covered her head turban-style, and the redness around her collar didn't look so pronounced now her skin had gained a rosy glow from her hot bath.

"Hello," she said, walking to the kitchen table with small steps and sitting with her back to the wall.

"Hello." Harry smiled and took the food-filled plate to her, setting it on a mat and placing a knife and fork either side. "I suspect you're hungry?"

She nodded and ignored the cutlery, picking up a hunk of bread and stuffing half of it into her mouth.

Where the devil had she come from? He turned away so she couldn't see his deepening frown, could eat in peace without the embarrassment of him watching. He busied himself making hot chocolate, taking an overly long time to stir each drink so he could compose himself. Something about her tugged at him, made him want to rush over and crush her to his chest, but he sensed his attentions wouldn't be received too well. What woman—dressed as she was, in the house of a stranger—would accept a hug from a man she didn't know?

He sighed deeply, blowing air out in a long, quiet stream, and picked up the steaming cups. With his gaze averted, he placed a cup before her and sat opposite, staring at the kitchen door in a bid to make her feel comfortable in his presence. He watched her from the corner of his eye, noting raised scars on her forearms, as though she'd been wounded with a knife. Or had she done that? Did she self-harm?

"I can see you looking, you know," she said, lifting the triangle of quiche and holding it in front of her mouth. "And yes, someone did that to me."

He whipped his head around at her confession, and she blushed, taking a large bite and looking at the back door.

"I think," she added quickly after swallowing. "I mean, I saw these scars when I was in the bath and just assumed someone had hurt me. It's not like I know for definite or anything."

She was playing him for a damn fool, he was sure of it, and who could blame her if she was running from someone who had made those hideous marks? But he wouldn't allow this charade to continue. If she wanted to stay, she would have to admit she hadn't lost her memory, and if it meant him threatening to oust her from his home, then he would do it, guilt be damned.

"You may as well just admit it," he said, raising his cup to his lips and avoiding eye contact...for now. He took a sip then cradled the cup in his lap. "It's in your best interests, after all. It means you get to stay longer."

"Fuck!" she said, dropping the quiche to her plate.

He winced at her language, his suspicion that she wasn't a woman from his circles confirmed. Oh, he wasn't averse to bad language. Far from it—he enjoyed using it and hearing it in the bedroom—but he wasn't used to women he dated using it in everyday speech.

But this isn't a date, so what does it matter how she speaks?

"Come on," he said gently. "It's obvious you have a Master. You may as well tell me about it—him, your situation. Perhaps I can help."

She snorted and picked up her fork, toying with the cuts of meat. "What the hell would you know about Masters?"

He smiled, took a sip of his drink and eyed her over the cup rim. "More than you might think."

She widened her eyes, realisation dawning, and let her fork go. It landed on the plate with a clatter, and she stared at him open-mouthed. "Oh, fuck me. Don't tell me you're a bloody Master?"

He almost choked on his chocolate. "I am, and I sense yours isn't a good one."

She lifted her hand to her collar and stared at the back door again.

"I also suspect that collar should come off. Keeping one placed about your neck by a deviant isn't advisable. Have you been mistreated?"

He knew she had, but his question was to get her to open up, not to just nod absently like she was doing now.

"Do you even know the proper rules?" He watched her eyes cloud over, as though memories had taken all her attention.

She tensed, fidgeting with that collar so harshly her nails scraped the skin of her neck.

"Please, stop doing that. You're going to hurt yourself."

"Felt worse pain than this," she whispered, lowering her hand and embracing herself around her middle.

"I have no doubt you have. Do you wish to talk about it?"

The floodgates opened then, and she related horrors no person should have to endure, all the while keeping her gaze fixed on that back door. He imagined her running, finally breaking free, the bite of the cold on her feet, the wind whipping her hair and freezing her body. He resisted the urge to get up and embrace her, resisted even making the simple gesture of reaching across the table to touch her arm, worrying any action may spook her.

"I knew all along he was a wrong'un," she said, tears wetting her cheeks. "Knew I shouldn't be there, pretending to be a damn lady when I wasn't and never will be. But he told me...he said that was the way a Dominant and submissive behaved, that I had to do whatever he told me whether I liked it or not. I'd read a bit about it in books, you know, when I worked in the library, but he said that was all a load of bollocks, that the books were wrong..."

She swiped her eyes with the back of one hand, and he was struck by the fact her tears were silent, no sobs accompanying them, no hitches of breath or the thickening of her voice. Had she been conditioned so much she was even afraid to cry?

Who the hell is this man?

"It's possible I may know him," he said, startled that he'd voiced his thoughts.

"Which is why I won't tell you his name. It's bad enough I've run from him—and he'll come looking for me, you can bet on that—but to have you confronting him, if that's what you had in mind... No, it'd make things worse for me." She shivered and unlocked her arms, reaching for her drink only to hold it to her chest.

"You might want to drink that before it gets cold," he said, leaving the subject of her Master's name behind them for now. "You've had quite an ordeal, and being out in the snow won't have helped." He ploughed on, "Do you wish to stay here for a while until you feel safe enough to find a place of your own? I assume you're not planning to return to him."

She shook her head. "I'm not going back—ever—and I don't rightly know what I'm going to do. I can't work at the library again—he'll look for me there—so maybe I ought to bugger off to another town or something, get completely away."

"Maybe."

He stood slowly and walked into the laundry room. The quick wash he'd set her clothes on had finished, and he transferred them to the dryer. "Your clothes will be ready soon," he said as he returned to the kitchen. "Shall we go into the living room so you can warm up a little more? I'm worried you might suffer from a chill and want you as warm as possible."

She cocked her head, giving him a quizzical look, as though his concern was utterly foreign to her, and he guessed that it undoubtedly was.

"I don't know why you'd give much of a shit, but yes, that would be nice."

He let her walk ahead of him and smiled at her word choice. Despite her way of speaking having initially made him cringe, he found her openness, her honest answers, refreshing. Especially since she'd now given him a brief description of her life prior to finding herself here. That she felt comfortable enough with him to revert back to her old ways was a step in the right direction. Her Master hadn't completely cowed her, hadn't stripped her of everything she'd been before she'd met the hateful man, and that was something to be grateful for.

In the living room, she sat at one end of the sofa while he sat at the other, close enough to see her facial expressions but far enough away to give her space. She stared at the fire, cup still nestled at her chest, and he studied her through lowered lashes, surprised he found her quite attractive. She wasn't his usual choice. He had a penchant for blondes with a few layers of fat on their bones, but her face appealed to him, her waif-like body bringing out his urge to nurture.

"I can explain a little about the proper rules, if you like?" he asked. With their sexual leanings in common, at least they had something to discuss. "About how play should be directed. It really isn't what your Master led you to believe. In other circumstances I'd offer to show you, to take you on as my sub until you'd learned all the rules, but with the state you're in, I really don't think it's advisable. You're vulnerable and, well…"

"I don't think I could handle a spanking tonight," she said, turning a weak smile his way. "Besides, you'd think me a right tart if I agreed, and I don't fancy being labelled as something else I'm not. I mean,

Master… He said I was all sorts of nasty things." She gave the fire her attention again.

"I wouldn't think you a tart. There's nothing wrong in two people indulging if they're both consenting. My concern is more about playing while you're vulnerable and unsure of the rules. It isn't my style to prey on women susceptible to upset due to their emotions being a little topsy-turvy."

She laughed, not unkindly, and looked his way again. "Topsy-turvy?"

He sensed she was gently mocking his way of speech, but that was okay. If it meant she laughed and smiled like that, he'd let her do it all the time. She was like a constantly kicked puppy — all the instinctual bite thrashed out of her — although he thought, given the chance, the right environment, and the right Master, her bite and her bark might be encouraged to return. How sad that she'd been reduced to someone so unsure, where one moment she was lost in her thoughts and the next a smidgen of her former, true self tried to penetrate through the person she had been forced to become.

He wondered whether he should take her on, encourage her to be who she really was. Would she even want that on the back end of such a traumatic D/s relationship? He shook his head. What was he doing? He should never have even thought about it. Ridiculous to expect her to jump into something new when old wounds still lay exposed and festering, still raw and open to infection. But, God…he had a hankering to mend this broken bird, to watch her fly with new wings and soar through a sky void of mean, dark clouds and storms.

"Tell me a bit," she said, cheeks flushing. "Tell me what I should have had, so next time—if there is a next time—I'll know what to expect."

She dug her elbow into the settee arm and rested her chin in her hand, her gaze fixed firmly on the rug in front of the fire. Harry frowned, thinking a little conversation wouldn't hurt. But maybe it would.

"If I tell you how it's supposed to be, won't you feel upset that you didn't have that?" he asked.

"Not really. Everyone has at least one shitty relationship—don't they?—and that was mine. We've all got to move on, learn to trust new people. I'm not stupid, I know damn well there will be things that set me off, remind me of him, but fucking hell, I can't live the rest of my life all scared and whatever, can I?"

He sensed she was covering up the pain with her bright tone, but if him talking went some way to helping, talk he would.

* * * *

"Wow," she said quietly when he'd finished. "So if I was your pupil, you'd *want* me to speak up, to tell you what I wanted?"

"Of course. How else is your Master to know what your threshold is? It isn't a Master's right to override your desires, more that he must accommodate them, incorporate them into play and enjoy making you happy, meeting your needs. This…this person you've been involved with used you for his own ends. I'm sorry if that hurts, but I can't allow you to go along thinking he was correct in what he did. It also sounds to me that he's naturally controlling, because to strip away your identity, to manipulate things so you're only reliant on him... That's a dangerous man to be involved with."

He looked at her to gauge her reaction, to see how much he could say without tipping her over the edge. Who knew what she had in her mind, what images played over and over, what emotions roiled inside her, set to send her crazy the moment she let down her guard and allowed herself to remember? She appeared awed, not devastated, though — the latter being how he'd thought she would react. It seemed she was more resilient than he'd given her credit for, although he wasn't fool enough to think she wouldn't suffer from the horrors she'd been through. It would take time to fully cherish this tiny woman, to have her totally believing what he said and understanding that she hadn't been the one in the wrong.

He found himself admitting he rather relished the idea of being the one to bring her out of herself, to watch her blossom under his tutelage.

Don't, Harry. It's a big undertaking. And who's to say she'd even want that?

As though she'd read his mind, she said, "Tomorrow, I want you to show me. I want us to do some mock play where you instruct me on the way it goes, what happens."

He opened his mouth to protest, disliking the squirm of nerves in his belly that he would be taking advantage of her.

"No," she said. "I might be hurting, I might have things in my head I shouldn't bloody well have, but I want to learn. Just pretend I'm someone from that club you told me about, someone you're taking on — you the teacher, me the pupil. It'll be all right, honest. I just want to see how it's really meant to be, because then it'll help me get over this shit. Then I'll understand and no bastard can hurt me ever again."

"But you hardly know me," he protested, thinking her mad to want to succumb to another Master so quickly.

"Doesn't matter. I can tell you're not a prick."

He bit back a laugh but couldn't prevent a smile twitching one corner of his mouth. "All right, but first I want to remove that collar. Would that be all right?"

She nodded, and he was pleased to see she didn't touch it. He stood and walked to his sideboard, opening a drawer and extracting a large, sharp pair of scissors. He had no idea how else to remove it.

He returned to the settee and sat beside her. "I don't think I have anything else I can use to take it off. I can only hope me sliding these between the collar and your neck won't cause too much distress."

She eyed him, then tilted her head. "Do it. Take the fucking thing off."

She closed her eyes—so much trust there—and he gently eased one blade of the scissors beneath the collar. It indented her neck, but thankfully, with the leather being thin, he was able to snip it quickly. He let it fall into her lap, and she opened her eyes to stare down at it.

"Get it off me?" she asked, hands held up as if it might taint her if she touched it again.

Harry pulled it off her lap. "Would you like me to dispose of it?"

She nodded, closing her eyes again, and he stood, walked over to the wicker waste bin and dropped the collar inside.

To take the sting from the monumental thing she had allowed him to do, he said brightly, "How about tomorrow I take you out, get you some new clothes?"

She snapped her head to face him, widening her eyes.

He raised a hand to stop her saying anything. "We'll go shopping in another town if that makes you feel better, have a nice day out, and then, after we've eaten dinner, we can begin your first lesson. How does that sound?"

She blew out a breath, straightening her shoulders. "Bloody brilliant. Here's to tomorrow, the first day of my new life."

Chapter Four

Ruby couldn't believe she was about to go shopping with a complete stranger — couldn't believe she was staying in his house, either. He sat opposite her in his kitchen sipping his morning coffee. The posh man had Italian blended coffee beans, which had to be ground and then filtered. Aromatic coffee scent surrounded them, and Ruby found the smell pleasant but the taste foul. Maybe it was her council roots, but she'd be happy with supermarket home-brand instant — a bitter taste but decent on the pocket.

"Could you pass the butter, please?" he asked.

Butter? What happened to good old-style margarine? Ruby knew deep down she was way out of her depth. She'd thought Master was upper class and posh, but this man really had it all about him. Even in the way he sat — his back straight, not slouched as he gazed down at the newspaper. Charm, confidence and sexual masculinity oozed from every move, pore and presence.

Yep, out of her depth.

"Which pot would that be?" From where she came from, marg was taken straight from the tub, no faff of transferring it from a perfectly reasonable tub to a pot because it looked pretty. Seriously, who had the time?

Harry chuckled, leaned over and took a weird-looking thing with a lid, which he lifted to reveal the slab of rich butter.

So now she knew the weird-looking pot with a lid now contained butter.

"You can eat anything you like," he said. "It looks like you could use more meat on your bones."

Was he taking the piss? She was fat all over. Master had monitored her eating habits. The bastard had even put chains on the fridge and cupboards so she couldn't snack while he was out. He'd fed and clothed her...and controlled every little way of her life. She raised her hand to her neck to touch the collar that had contained her for so long, only to find a bare expanse of neck. Master kept all the keys to her freedom on a little chain at his waist—the one to her collar just another to keep her with him.

"The coffee will do," she said, not willing to risk another pound to her weight.

"This isn't something your Master was teaching you, was he? You do realise you're underweight? You look pale and fragile and really need some food."

Each one of his words sounded like the truth, but years of constant verbal and mental abuse from the man who claimed to love her had filled her with self-doubt. She'd been taken over, had insecurity ingrained inside her from his brainwashing.

"He did, didn't he? Another one of his little control games?" Harry asked gently.

Ruby watched him fist the newspaper and she flinched. After so many times of watching hands fist in the same way, only to be struck moments later...it was all still so clear in her mind.

He cursed. Ruby gazed at him in wonder — the curse so shocking it took her out of her fear and instantly brought on surprise. She hadn't expected to hear a word like that from him. He got up from his seat, placing his paper down on the table, and went to his knees in front of her. She refused to back away from him. He wouldn't hurt her. Despite knowing that on a subconscious level, she kept chanting calming words inside her head — force of habit. Sweat beaded on her forehead — why, when she wasn't scared, she didn't know — and she tried to keep her shaking hands contained in her lap.

Ruby expected him to touch her, lash out at her. Instead, he looked at her. He saw right through her, she was sure of it, past the waves of insecurity and the battle she fought to be the fun-loving Ruby with him — previous name remaining a secret — to the shell of a human being she became under the hard lessons from Master.

"You're terrified, I can see it," he said. "I don't usually curse. I'm sorry if I frightened you."

Harry appeared deep in thought, and all Ruby wanted to do was reach out and reassure him. But something was stopping her. In her heart of hearts she knew he wouldn't hurt her, and part of her loved her new name simply because Harry, her white knight, had given it to her. But if she lifted a hand, touched him, and took away the distance, what more would she open herself up to?

"I'd never hurt you. In all my life as a Dom, I've never struck a single female or any of my subs in anger or for proper punishment. I adore them for the pleasure and trust they grant me with their minds and bodies."

He took one of her shaking hands in his. Ruby let out a rush of breath she didn't even know she'd been holding. His touch was firm but not painful. He held her gently, as though he was of the old-fashioned mindset—he was the man and she a woman to be taken care of. There was nothing threatening in his action, he merely offered her comfort. With no further speech, he allowed her to become accustomed to the simple act of him grasping her hand. Unable to resist, she stared into his eyes, trying to see if she could read his intentions. He stared right back.

What was he thinking? What was he feeling? Did his hand warm or tingle from her touch or was it a simple gesture of consolation?

The act of kindness flowed through her mind. Master had fucked her over harder than she'd ever realised. How long had she been with him? Three years? Longer? And in all that time—once she'd moved in with him—she couldn't recall a tender touch, kiss or caress. No kind words of comfort. Bitch, slut, whore, filth—all the degrading words that had filled her days. Nothing had ever been good enough or right. Every punishment had been exactly that—a punishment meant to hurt, not to enhance their love life.

It suddenly dawned on Ruby—since meeting Master and being in his life, she hadn't experienced a proper orgasm since the first one she'd had, on the night she'd moved in. The terrifying ordeal she'd been through after climaxing without permission had taken their budding relationship into a downward spiral she'd had no chance of ever escaping. At least now Ruby could admit that if she hadn't got away, she'd be leaving her old room at Master's in a body bag...or worse, dead, dumped outside in his back yard.

Ruby shivered and averted her gaze from the man who was demanding access into her head, the very soul of her being. Through it all, Master had never fully conquered her mind. For the longest time she'd thought of escape, forming the best-laid plan. Her escape had worked, and as she sat here now, trying to avoid Harry's penetrating gaze, she couldn't help but be relieved by her random luck on him finding her.

He caressed her palm with his thumb, rotating little circles over her skin, the touch nice and gentle after so much pain. Ruby leaned her head back and closed her eyes in bliss, loving the contact of another person who didn't have plans to harm her. He circled her wrist, fingers strong, bringing her right back to how she'd felt with Master. His finger and thumb touched, his grip tightening, and the sudden feeling of being trapped brought her up short. She yanked her hand from his grip, drawing her delicate and easily breakable wrist to her chest.

"You're skin and bone, Ruby." He spoke softly, his hand falling to her thigh.

Ruby glanced at his hand but didn't pull away, even though she wanted to be alone, far from the fear of an outburst of anger. At the same time she craved the touch, the intimacy from him.

He represented peace.

"I'm fine," she whispered.

Her stomach decided to tell the man otherwise, letting out a huge growl.

Fucking feed me.

A blush spread over her face and neck. She wanted him to feed her and wondered if she would allow it if he did. Harry smiled, resting his hand on her stomach.

"Eat something for me," he said.

Each touch he gave was clearly designed to calm and soothe her.

Ruby nodded. He took a ripe, juicy piece of peach from a bowl and raised it to her lips. She obliged him, opening her mouth and taking the chunk. The melting sweetness burst on her tongue, and she couldn't stop the moan of approval.

"That's good. Take another bite."

Harry continued to feed her bite-size chunks of fruit and toast until her tummy suddenly stopped rumbling and she held her hand up for him to stop. She was amazed by how patient he was. From looking at his face, Ruby couldn't decipher what he was thinking or feeling. Nothing about his presence gave anything away, but she could see, *feel* he would never hurt her. With Master, she'd memorised certain movements and sounds that let her know beforehand his type of mood—whether he wanted to lash out and hurt, or bring torture, or just plain taunt her. With Harry she didn't know anything about him except for the unmistakable air of kindness, the times he was a little too posh, and his soft sarcasm last night in the upstairs hallway.

Once she was finished eating, she sipped the foul-tasting coffee—tiny sips to appease him. Harry tapped her knee and moved to the other end of the table. Ruby admired him more for not expecting anything from her.

For giving her time and personal space.

"Ruby, thank you for eating breakfast. You gave me great pleasure in feeding you." He picked up his own coffee.

She frowned. "I don't understand. You *want* me to eat? To put on weight?"

There was more going on with him than Ruby was comfortable with. She couldn't get her head around the contrast between the two men.

"You've never been thanked by your Master before, have you?"

What could she say? Master was a first-class prick — not that she'd ever say it to his face.

"Let's just say he was bigger on the punishments and verbal abuse than he ever was on being nice." Without thinking, she took a huge gulp of coffee, the taste hitting her throat, making her heave. Turning away from him as best she could, she spat the liquid back into her cup.

She expected some sort of anger.

"You don't like the coffee?" He sipped his with a raised eyebrow.

One day, she'd shave that thing off if he wasn't careful.

"It's disgusting. Tastes like horse shit, not that I know what horse shit tastes like."

"No need to be vulgar. It's Italian blend."

Unable to raise just one eyebrow herself, Ruby raised both of hers.

"You're right. There is no need to be vulgar and I apologise. I'm more of an instant-coffee person."

Fucking think before you speak. Don't say shit like that.

"I'll remember for next time on the coffee detail," he said. "So you've never been complimented?"

Ruby shook her head.

"Right. Seeing as you asked me to show you how a Master should behave and actually teach you the ways in a proper relationship, I'll begin now. My belief and teaching is to treat my submissive with the utmost respect and let her know when she's doing something that pleases me. You pleased me by eating, and I thanked you for it."

Everything he'd said so far had made sense. She waited for him to continue.

"I've been thinking. You really struggle with me being close, and I thought of a good way to show you the building of trust within a Dom and submissive partnership."

Ruby was intrigued and leaned further on the table to listen. Before her time with Master, she'd been interested in learning more about BDSM.

"You've clearly had a bad time, and I think using a safe word now, outside of the bedroom, will show you that no matter what, I would never ever hurt you."

"I don't understand."

"As soon as a safe word is decided and agreed upon, you'll use it from here on. What I'm proposing is if I ever scare you or make you uncomfortable in a way you don't like, you'll say a safe word. For instance, 'butter'. If you say the word 'butter' when you're not comfortable with me or are frightened, I'll stop and change. This will show you how being a submissive is empowering to the mind and body, that you have control over what I say or do. That it is a partnership," Harry said.

Ruby nibbled her lip. Before, Master had ignored her safe word and continued regardless of the rules. She looked down at her knotted fingers—interlocked, as though trying to protect themselves from an enemy they didn't deserve. For too long Master had been the voice inside her head, and if she didn't break free soon, she'd be forever in his grasp.

Holding a hand out across the table, she shook Harry's.

"Deal."

"And the safe word?" he asked.

Ruby smiled. "Let's stick with butter."

Her heart jolted as he smiled back, nodding in agreement.

He truly was a handsome man.

* * * *

Ruby had decided on the spur of the moment to throw caution to the wind and shop in Manchester, not another nearby town as Harry had suggested. She'd have to face Master at some point, and although she didn't relish it today, with Harry by her side she had more confidence. Besides, Master rarely went into the city. He ordered what he needed online or sent one of his employees out for purchases.

They'd been shopping for hours, Ruby wearing a pair of Harry's black wellingtons that were too big and a coat that drowned her. He'd soon remedied that, buying her a pair of boots that fitted and a thick red jacket to die for. A scarf and gloves too. She thought her feet were going to fall off from all the walking and changing of clothes. What was wrong with seeing a shirt or trousers in the colour you liked, trying one set on and then leaving with the same style in a variety of different colours? According to Harry...everything. Every shirt, pair of trousers, skirt, dress, all types of shoes and lingerie needed to be tried on.

And not only that, he wanted to check for himself that they fitted perfectly.

The lingerie, though...he allowed her to pick that herself without showing him. The perfect gentleman. He chose some clothes and waited for her to try them on. The saleswomen were falling over their feet giving him everything he wanted and vying for his attention. There was clearly power with money and good looks. Harry was sexy after all—even she couldn't deny the appeal and attraction.

Throughout the day, her body came alive whenever he was near, shocking considering what she'd been through, but part of her was still a young, red-blooded woman.

"You need stilettos with that dress, Ruby." He turned to the young assistant. "Stacey, honey. I say—the red pair over there. Could you fetch them?"

"You're aware you barely know me and you're buying a shitload of clothes for me." She rested her hand on her hip. The tight, silky dress felt wonderful, clinging to every curve and joint, but she turned in the mirror and wondered why women dressed like it all the time. Shirts and trousers for everyday wear and comfort and she was set.

"It gives me pleasure to spend money on you." He leant back on the large sofa dominating the changing area.

"Yeah, for all you know I could be feeding you a load of rubbish and taking you for a ride for your money."

"If that's the case, for all you know I could be the gardener or the house sitter."

Touché.

The set-up between them was bizarre to say the least, but for some reason Ruby was drawn to him unlike any other man.

The woman handed her the heels and Ruby put them on.

"Leave us," Harry told the assistant.

Ruby turned back to look in the mirror. Harry stood directly behind her. She let out a gasp, shocked for the first time in years to not be afraid *at all*. She'd spent the better part of three hours with him trying on clothes and watching him laugh and was comfortable in his presence. While waiting for clothes in different sizes, they'd started to talk about their hobbies. Ruby had given nothing away about her private name and previous address but had talked about what she liked and what she didn't.

Harry said he enjoyed long walks through the country when he got the time, swimming, and listening to classical music in his office while getting a rub from a very famous local masseuse. He read murder mysteries and thrillers in his spare time, which wasn't a lot, and collected different wines. Not a fan of television, he loved the theatre, opera and going to the movies.

He was a Dominant through and through, and if she looked closely she could see it with her own eyes. His demand for attention with his softly spoken words made women and men comply. He had many years of experience, and he used it to his advantage. Always calm and ready.

She, however, had told him pretty much nothing. The long walks were the same. It seemed very surreal when he'd asked her what she liked. For so long she'd schooled herself to like nothing, to wish for nothing, and now she was having to find who she was again.

What did she like to read, listen to, or talk about? There were simple things she could tell him, like stuff she enjoyed eating and the walking, but all the other hobbies and somewhat mundane things were lost to her.

Every time she realised how much the bastard from her previous life had affected her, the more upset she became.

"You look ravishing," Harry whispered right behind her, her back touching his front, his presence not enough to crowd but enough for her to know he was there.

"Th-thank you." Ruby wished she could tell him something, anything about herself that he would find interesting. "I'm sorry," she mumbled, looking away from his eyes in the mirror.

He touched her shoulder, and instead of pulling away she spun and rested her head on his chest, seeking the comfort and safety of his touch.

"Why are you sorry?" he asked, stroking her hair.

Tears fell, wetting his shirt—she couldn't contain them. "I don't know who I am anymore. I was someone with hobbies and passions, and now I feel like a dead shell." Ruby couldn't even sob now. Tears continued to fall as though crying was a passing thought.

How many times had she lain in bed or on the floor and the tears had simply seeped? Too many to count and too morbid to even think of counting.

Harry lifted her chin with a finger, tilting her head so she gazed at him.

"You should never be sorry. The monster who did this to you should be sorry. You'll find yourself again, Ruby, and I'll help you every step of the way."

She smiled and wound her hands around his neck, cuddling against his body. He held her, too, hands at her hips.

For so long in this terrifying world she'd been alone, expecting to brave it alone. It was nice to have a lifeline and possibly a friend to hold on to. It was strange, but for many years Ruby had pictured a man like Harry—gentle and kind, a man she could fall for. Like, fall in love with, in a big way. She spent so many hours stuck in a library, seeing either older men or stuffy, spotty teenagers with attitude. Hunting for or even believing in Mr Right had been off the agenda for some time. What would it be like to love a man like Harry? She wasn't averse to his touch — she welcomed it, which was another shock.

"You're a strong woman, Ruby, and one day you'll see and prove to me exactly how strong you are, and in doing so, you'll get your life back."

His words were a promise, and she reacted by snuggling more closely, inhaling his scent that was becoming addictive to her.

She switched her thoughts to what he had said, the gift he had given her, more precious than the clothes and shoes — butter, her safe word…and she knew in her heart and mind she'd never use it with him.

Harry was a different type of man. He was a keeper.

* * * *

"I've not had fish and chips in years." Harry stood at her back in the crowded fish and chips bar.

Harry had suggested they go for a walk to some fancy French restaurant. Ruby hated French food — snails, frogs…*yuk* — so walking past this busy chip shop had been a welcoming distraction.

"So you'll enjoy them," she said. "A true British staple — a bag of fish 'n' chips."

He snorted.

She burst out laughing. "Stop being so damn posh and embrace your common side."

His hands circled her waist, and he nuzzled her neck, making her giggle again. The touches and rapport between them were so natural, Ruby couldn't stop smiling, and it was nice to finally relax and lean on his shoulders.

They waited in line, silent, and Ruby got the chance to look around her, part of her keeping an eye out for Master. She would always be on alert in case he showed, though she just wanted to enjoy being with Harry.

She spotted a couple ahead of them in the queue — the woman turned towards her man. She smiled at something he was saying, and he tilted his head and kissed her.

Ruby gasped. Her toes curled within her boots, her nipples hardened and cream gathered in her panties. The affection they had towards each other was affecting her body. It had been so long since the flood of warmth had happened involuntarily between her legs that she blushed, her face hot and prickly.

"What's the matter?" Harry asked.

Ruby showed him the couple as discreetly as she could.

"What about them?" Harry did his trick of only raising one eyebrow.

"They look so lovely together. I wonder what it would be like to be kissed with affection, love, and to have someone care enough to make sure you liked it?" Her sigh was filled with longing.

"You mean like this?"

He took her chin and tilted her head back. Before she could stop or analyse anything, his lips covered hers. Ruby closed her eyes and embraced his touch, the feelings he inspired in her. His lips pressed, firm but lovely, and he ran his tongue along her lip seam, coaxing her to open to him. She couldn't refuse and parted her lips to better receive him. His tongue glided inside and melded with her own.

It wasn't an act, wasn't just a casual kiss, and the heat bloomed within her. Ruby gave everything over to him, letting him take control and meeting him halfway, other people in the queue be damned.

This is what it's like to be kissed? I never want this to end...

"Love birds, what's your order?"

A tap on her arm jerked her back to the present. The couple behind them were urging them forward. The queue in front had dispersed.

"What can I get you?" the woman behind the counter asked.

Ruby looked at her dumbfounded. Harry had just kissed her. On the lips. And she had liked it. His hands still circled her waist. *Her* hands shook as she ran her fingers through her hair. Lips tingling, she licked them, hoping to taste him.

Could she allow their relationship to go further? Could she let him teach her then walk away? Or was she better off staying at Harry's to lick her wounds then moving on alone, far away from Master?

"Well, lady, what's it going to be?"

The question in her mind was two-edged. On the one hand the lady was asking for her order, but in her mind she was asking herself the very same question but for an entirely different reason.

What was it going to be?

Ruby gazed up at Harry, and he smiled down at her, running a thumb over her lips.

"Your choice," he said. "I'd like you to choose what we eat."

She swallowed the sudden lump in her throat, one that had burgeoned from yet another gift from him.

The chance to have her own voice.

"Two fish and chips, please. Salt and vinegar as well," she replied, and in her heart and mind she answered her own question.

No matter how scary or new this thing was with Harry, she was going to see it through to the fullest and fight the demons of her past.

Master, for all intents and purposes, could go and fuck himself.

Chapter Five

Master slammed down the telephone, paced his living room and fumed. His heart rate soared to dangerous levels, making it difficult to breathe without his chest hurting. If Margaret was here he would have taken his ire out on her—a few lashes with a stout walking cane would have done the trick—but a night had passed with still no sign of her. Where was she? Why hadn't she returned? He thought he'd conditioned her enough so she would have slunk back with her tail between her legs before now. And why had the damn snow fallen so fast when he'd searched for her last night, as though the fates were against him? It had obliterated her footsteps in no time, leaving him at a loss as to where to go once he reached the end of his quiet street.

He grimaced. She'd *so* pay for this disobedience.

He'd ordered a specialised piece of equipment last week and it had yet to arrive, hence the phone call to the supplier. The rude male shop assistant told him he could collect it if his need was so urgent, his words full of sarcasm, giving Master the impression the chap wasn't particularly fussed at his threat to take his business elsewhere after a refund. The snow had prevented any vans going out, surely Master understood that.

Master bristled, clamping his jaw tight. It didn't matter to the shop assistant whether his need was urgent. The delivery should have been with him days ago, snow or not — a delivery that would have stopped Margaret running out on him.

"Damn it!" he muttered, walking to the window and looking out.

His front garden appeared nothing more than an expanse of untouched white, the road, too. No cars had driven down the street today, and it seemed people in the homes opposite hadn't ventured out, their snow-covered lawns free of gouges from footprints. He didn't blame them, he hadn't had any intention of going out himself today if it weren't for that blasted delivery and his need to have his purchase in place for when Margaret returned.

Would the contraption even fit in his Land Rover? He thought about the size of it once erected, what it had looked like when he'd browsed online, and suspected it must come in pieces. He'd have to build it himself, and this time last week he'd relished the prospect of seeing Margaret held in place by it, unable to leave the room unless he unlocked the straps and allowed her some freedom. Today, he revelled in thinking of her locked up and never being free, never knowing any other place but the room he'd planned to use for her incarceration times. And it was all her fault. If she hadn't run, he'd have only locked her up as a treat, a few hours here and there, but when she came back…

She'll never leave this house again. Until I'm tired of her.

A fresh surge of annoyance oozed through him at the image of her floating inside his head, all smiling face and smug expression. He heard her voice, the unmistakeable triumph in it. *"I'm free, Master."*

He pursed his lips, clenched his hands and left the living room, knowing he had no alternative but to go out into that terrible weather and collect the item he was desperate for. And he *was* desperate. Yes, he was desperate to erect it and desperate to bind her to it.

Little bitch.

Shrugging into his coat and pulling on boots he wouldn't usually be seen dead in, he left the house, stepping straight into knee-deep snow. His trousers would be wet in no time—he hadn't been so crass as to tuck them into his boots, that just wouldn't do for his image—and the cold was already seeping through the fabric.

"Goddamn you, Margaret!"

He struggled towards the garage door, standing still for a moment to wonder how the buggery he was going to get rid of the snow in front of it. He clicked a button on his key fob and hoped the automatic door was strong enough to shift the snow for him. It was, although he got a good dusting of the white stuff in the process. Snow sneaked past his coat collar and melted on his neck. He bit back a string of curses and tromped inside the garage, never more thankful to own a vehicle that would have no issues navigating the thick snow.

Once inside, he belted up and whacked on the heater.

"Margaret, you *will* be grateful for all the trouble I'm going to this afternoon."

He started the engine then reversed — pleased he made it out onto the street without incident. He clicked the garage key fob again, waited for the door to close, then drove down his street slowly — not good for his current mood, which demanded speed and the reckless taking of corners, tyres screeching. Instead, the tyres compacted the snow, the resulting crunch of sound oddly loud over the engine in the otherwise creepy quiet.

It felt as though the end of the world had come and he was the sole survivor.

He smiled at that.

I am *a survivor.*

Buoyed by that thought, he made the painfully slow trip into town, happy to see more cars and life once he'd left the estate where he lived. The main roads had been cleared, peach-coloured grit mixed with grey slush covering the tarmac, and banks of dirty snow sat hunched at the kerbs, uneven and unpleasant to the eye.

The multi-storey car park, virtually empty, meant Master had a wide variety of spaces to choose from. He stuck to the ground floor — easier to bring his contraption there from the shop, the stairs and elevator would prove a bind — and walked with half his mind on his forthcoming argument with the rude shop assistant and half on the treacherous, slippery pathways leading to the shopping centre.

He reached one set of three double glass doors and pushed inside, the blast of warmth welcome after the biting cold. He stamped his feet on the wide ribbed mat and noted the cleaners hadn't been vigilant in mopping up the melted snow that had fallen from shoppers' boots, wet streaks and footprints abundant on the white tiles.

What was the world coming to when people didn't do the job they were paid for?

He walked through at a brisk pace, dodging other shoppers and heading for the doors right at the other end. The shop he sought was opposite the centre in a side street people rarely walked down. It appeared to be merely a small store that sold women's lingerie, vibrators and the like, but in reality it sold much, much more for the BDSM customer.

As he approached the exit, a woman outside in a bright red jacket caught his attention. There was something about the way she moved that reminded him of Margaret when he'd first met her. She had her back to him and walked in delicious high-heeled boots towards a rubbish bin, balled up paper in one hand. Hmmm. Perhaps he would follow her, see if she was alone, and accidentally bump into her to strike up a conversation. It wouldn't hurt to become acquainted, exchange numbers, to have another woman waiting in the wings in case Margaret didn't come back.

The dawn of a new challenge rose inside him, and his cock twitched at the thought of seducing another woman and teaching her exactly how she should behave. That would have to wait, though. He had unfinished business with Margaret, and he couldn't begin again until he'd settled the score, removed her collar and set her free. Of course, he'd make sure no other man at the club would want her. Make it clear she was bad news, a disobedient slut. His cock hardened a little at the idea of him telling fellow Doms all about Margaret and how she wasn't worth the shit on his shoe, their eyes wide and lips pursed that such a female existed—a woman who shunned a decent Dom's teachings the way she had.

He'd get her back, punish her severely, then ruin her.

At the doors, he lifted a palm to the glass ready to push one open, but was stopped short at the sight of Harry Knowles striding across the slushy path towards the bin where the woman in the red jacket stood. Master sighed, a heavy exhalation that seemed to come right from his soul. It stood to reason Knowles would bag a woman like her, and Master grimaced at the liberties the sub undoubtedly had with him. Knowles belonged to the group of club men who thought subs had the right to their own voice. Master and his friends regularly clashed with them—arguments rife during the monthly discussion times after new subs were introduced—and nothing ever got resolved, no stalemate was ever met. It was one of the reasons Master had never taken Margaret to the club. He didn't want Knowles and the like filling her head with insane information.

He stared through the glass, waiting for Knowles and the woman to walk away. She turned to face Knowles, a scarf wrapped loosely around her neck so he couldn't see if she wore Knowles' collar, the wool partially covering her face, but the slope of her nose made Master's stomach contract.

Margaret?

He cocked his head, red-hot bile surging up and heating the back of his tongue. He narrowed his eyes, forcing himself to see the woman more clearly, telling himself it had been a trick of his imagination. She faced the shopping centre, head thrown back as she laughed at something Knowles said—teeth on show, neck on show…minus a collar.

Margaret's teeth and neck.

Oh, no. That is not *acceptable. You ran from me to him?*

He had the urge to fly out there and confront them, reclaim Margaret and frogmarch her through the shopping centre and take her home, but he held off. There was another way to ensure she came back to him. He quickly formed a plan, biting back a cry of utter astonishment that she had possibly been seeing Knowles without his knowledge. For all his teachings, she'd clearly retained her original spirit, ignoring his warnings that once she accepted his collar, she was his until he said otherwise.

Who the hell do you think you are, slut?

And as for Knowles… He'd be having serious words with him.

Master trailed them for the rest of the afternoon, keeping an eye on the time so he could still collect his contraption. He needed it more than ever now.

Knowles played the perfect gentleman, guiding her with a hand to her elbow, holding the shopping bags and allowing her to walk through open doorways before he did. Master gritted his teeth, annoyed beyond measure that all his hard work was being unravelled so quickly. It made sense now, why, for the past fortnight or so, Margaret hadn't been doing everything she'd been told. Knowles had already got his oar in behind the scenes, making her think what Master did was wrong, and she'd rebelled, finally fleeing. Master rebuked himself for the smidgen of worry he'd felt at the thought of Margaret being outside in the cold all night. She hadn't been in the cold at all, but snuggled in Knowles' bed, lapping up his attention and probably telling him what she wanted and how.

It wouldn't only be Margaret who would pay, then.

Master kept a discreet distance at all times, and once, Margaret tensed, tilted her head and whipped around as though she sensed him there. He'd darted into a shop doorway before she had a chance to settle her gaze on him, and he smiled that he was still inside her head, their connection still in place.

You know I'm here, don't you, bitch?

She shuddered and turned to face ahead, Knowles whispering something, then linking her arm with his. The man questioned her, and she shook her head, glancing across to smile at him—a smile she hadn't bestowed upon Master since the very early days. A pinch of jealousy twanged then, to know he hadn't been able to elicit such a response from her for years. Yet it was her fault…again. If she hadn't been so bloody headstrong he would never have had to be strict with her.

After trailing the slut and Knowles up and down the centre for two hours, he pursued them out of the top-end doors where he'd first spotted them. His stomach clenched when he realised where they were headed — the sex shop where his contraption sat in the storeroom waiting for him to collect it. His blood boiled as he walked up the side street, the ground as snowy as his road, pedestrians not having been bothered to come along here. Their laughter drifted back to him—Margaret's a high peal when she slid on hidden ice, Knowles gripping her tightly so she didn't fall. Master wanted to bark out that if she weren't wearing ridiculous heels in this weather, she might not have had any trouble.

They disappeared inside the sex shop. Master positioned himself at the side of the window, giving himself enough space to see inside yet withdraw should either of them look out. Margaret fondled a paddle, and Master released a low grumble. She'd never liked paddles with him, claiming from the beginning that they hurt, made her want to cry because he hit her too hard. He'd shown her he hadn't hit hard enough and smacked her about the head with it.

She'd remained silent after that when he'd used the paddle again.

Knowles selected a crop with several leather straps and ran the strands over his palm, talking to Margaret and looking into her eyes the whole time. She shook her head and he replaced the crop on a hook, leading her further into the shop to look at other toys. She reached up and took a vibrator from the top shelf, modest in size and not nearly wide enough to stretch her mouth or cunt until they hurt. A coward's choice, one who wasn't into feeling pain and discomfort.

She still had so much to learn. There was still so much to teach her.

At her nod, Knowles took the vibrator and paid for it at the desk, producing a credit card with a flourish.

Master wanted to burst into the shop and break the man's neck.

Instead, he returned to the shopping centre, waiting at a window table in a café for the couple to walk past, then he went back to the sex shop. He had a satisfying argument with the sales assistant, which ended up with him getting a discount and being allowed to stack his contraption box on a trolley. After a painfully annoying time of trying to push it along the side street, he made it to his Land Rover, sure that Knowles and Margaret were long gone.

Box in his vehicle, he contemplated taking the trolley back to the shop as he'd promised but decided against it. Sitting in the driver's seat, he entertained thoughts of Margaret and Knowles, still somewhat shocked that they were together, although he was pleased to have noted she wore no collar. Although it signified she was done with Master, it also meant Knowles hadn't fully claimed her.

Good job, because she still belongs to me, missing collar or not.

He gunned the engine, reversed out of his spot, and drove home, the finer details of his plan slotting into place.

Chapter Six

Harry cleared away the remnants of their light supper—cheese, crackers and pickles—while Ruby relaxed in the bath. Her feet ached, she'd said, from their jaunt into the city, her not having walked so much in years. He stacked the plates in the dishwasher, a nugget of annoyance towards her Dom threatening to grow into so much more—anger, terrible anger that would consume him if he thought too hard for too long. Who the hell was the man who had treated her like that, and why wouldn't she tell him his name? He could understand her withholding that information, but by God, it wasn't as though he could find the fellow, storm over there and give him a good going over, was it? Harry knew the law too well for that. No, he'd just be content knowing his name so he could file it away for future use. Who knew? Ruby's former Master might need Harry's services one day and Harry would have much pleasure in denying him.

So much had happened today. His head reeled with memories, their kiss in the chip shop top of the list. That had been the last thing he'd expected to happen so soon after she'd escaped an abusive relationship, but the look in her eyes when she'd gazed at the couple in front of them had just about broken his heart. He'd wanted to give her what she'd always dreamed of—a kiss that curled her toes and made her feel wanted—and from the jolt of electricity that had speared through him as their lips touched, he could say with certainty he'd achieved that.

At times, more so in the afternoon, Ruby had seemed tense, admitting she felt uneasy, as though her Master were close. He'd told her she could hold his arm if it made her feel better, and she had. He'd taken much pleasure from that action, realising she was comfortable enough with him to do so. That she trusted, even if just a little bit. No one should go through what Ruby had, yet today, anyone looking at them would have naturally assumed they were a happy couple, together for quite some time.

How had that happened, the easy way they'd found with one another despite meeting less then twenty-four hours ago? Ruby telling him about herself last night had obviously brought them closer together, giving Harry an excess of information he'd have only usually gleaned after dating a woman for several weeks or months. They'd bypassed the to-and-fro dance of exchanging snippets, instead divulging most things about themselves in the space of a few hours.

He cleaned the sides with a wet cloth and swept the floor, even though it didn't need sweeping, just to waste some time until Ruby was finished. He must remember to call his cleaner, Gwen, and tell her not to bother coming in next week. She rode a bicycle to his house, and doing so in this weather wasn't safe. The same went for his gardener. A week off would do them both good anyway—they worked far too hard, this house and the grounds being too big for them to keep on top of. If the snow continued to fall, he wouldn't be going into the office Monday either. That wasn't a hardship, not with Ruby here to keep him company.

He wondered if the bath water had eased her aching muscles yet, or whether she'd fallen asleep cocooned in bubble-filled water scented with lilac and rosemary, the bath essence he'd bought for her today.

While out, he'd had the urge to pamper her, to buy everything in sight a woman might need or want, but although she'd allowed him to purchase a goodly amount, she'd made a point of telling him she'd pay back every penny when she was back on her feet.

He didn't want the money back. He just wanted to see her settled and happy, her head full of the knowledge that the sexual lifestyle she'd chosen wasn't to be one of horror or fear. He could only hope he'd save her in time, that her Master hadn't done too much damage, and that his teachings would override those that had come before.

The soft patter of her footsteps brought him out of his reverie. He propped the broom against the side and turned to see her standing in the doorway. She looked beautiful, if a little thin, in a black sheer gown, and he hoped that by her living here for a while her figure would soon fill out. She'd eaten the fish and chips earlier as though ravenous, and he'd felt for her going without enough food for so long.

He smiled and soaked in the sight of her. The tone of her skin, rosy from her bath, gave her a healthy glow and him the need to stroke it. She'd washed her hair, damp tendrils splayed over her chest, and he wondered whether he'd ever get the chance to hold it in his fist and tug, Ruby unafraid of what he was doing.

"Do you feel comfortable wearing that?" he asked, wanting to know whether his choice had been right, that she hadn't just agreed to the purchase to make him happy.

"Yes. I haven't been allowed to wear a negligee for a long time. I feel" — she blushed — "sexy."

"Good." He cleared his throat, the stirrings of desire beginning at the base of his cock. "Are you ready to begin what we discussed in the sex shop?" To stave off a full-on erection, he poured two glasses of white wine, then approached her, holding one out.

She took it, fingers brushing his. His cock jumped and he chewed the inside of his cheek. He didn't need a hard-on now, not when they were about to embark on something that might frighten and embarrass her.

"Yes," she said. "I think so." She bit her bottom lip.

His heart sped up. "If you're not certain…"

"No, no, I'm certain. It's just… You're only going to be my teacher, right?"

A glut of sadness and disappointment pooled in his gut, but he smiled reassuringly and said, "Yes, if that's how you want it to be."

He frowned at what he'd said. Hadn't that been the whole idea, him being her teacher then sending her on her way? Why, then, did it sting when she'd made that point clear? Did he want more from her, was that it? Oh, he'd been wanting a sub like her for some time, one who was willing to share her likes and dislikes with him instead of just being a yes-girl. But was he ready to become more seriously involved? With someone as broken as Ruby?

He was surprised to realise he was.

She sipped her wine then lowered the glass. "It's probably best that way, right? I mean, you're some hot-shot solicitor. You wouldn't want the likes of me hanging around for too long, and I — "

"Is that what you think?" He took a step forward and placed his fingers on her arm, wanting to touch yet not wanting to scare her with a full-on grip to her biceps as he would have done to any other woman.

"Well, stands to reason I'm not your type. We get on and all that, but... Look, I've got a runaway mouth on me, what with my swearing, and there's no way a bloke like you would want some common piece on his arm permanently. So yes, it's probably best that you teach me, make me understand what it's really all about, then I'll bugger off and leave you to it."

"I don't want you to bugger off," he blurted.

She widened her eyes and clutched her glass tighter, droplets of condensation trickling over her fingers. "Oh." She turned away then, head bowed, a frown firmly in place, and walked out of the room.

He'd gone too far, too quickly, hadn't he? Suddenly unsure whether to follow or give her space, he gulped some wine and considered the best course of action. Nothing had surprised him more than the speed with which he'd become attached to her. He thought about her leaving after her training was done and knew it would hurt. Was it her vulnerability, often covered with her brash words and fake bravado, that made him want to take care of her? Was it the way she was a breath of fresh air in that she said things exactly as she saw them, not thinking of how it might sound to him?

He supposed it was. And the latter? He was pleased she felt able to do that, because it obviously hadn't been allowed with her former Dom. She was honest, not out to snare him for his money, and he appreciated that trait after recent relationships had ended with the women revealing themselves to be gold diggers. Ruby was eager to learn, and he, in turn, was eager to teach. Until she expressed the admission she didn't want to bugger off either, he'd tell himself she was his pupil and nothing more.

Whether he believed his own lies remained to be seen.

* * * *

She sat before him on the rug, legs crossed, hands in the space between them. Her knees, shins and feet were on display, her negligee pooled beneath her fingers. She'd closed her eyes as he'd instructed, and the fire crackled behind her, drying her hair into crinkles.

"Now tell me what you want," he said. "The ultimate fantasy."

Her eyes flickered, and she parted her lips as though she was about to say something but had thought better of it. Or she wasn't brave enough or ready to tell him what he wanted to know.

"It doesn't matter that I'm sitting in front of you," he said. "The lamp doesn't show you too much—you're kind of in shadow. Pretend you're alone."

"It's difficult because I bloody *know* you're there!"

He smiled, holding back a chuckle. "If you want to learn…"

"All right, all right, keep your hair on!"

Laughter barked out of him before he could stop it, and she smiled, the self-conscious kind, and gripped the negligee hem. He felt for her, he really did, and wondered whether it was too soon for her to express herself when she was still so raw. That thought sobered him.

"I…" She sighed. "Sod it. How hard can it be?"

"Only as hard as you make it."

"Now that sounded rude…"

"It did, but it wasn't meant that way, I assure you."

"Shame."

She bunched her eyes tight, obviously cursing herself for letting her feelings slip out, but that one word gave him hope. Dare he dream she wanted him as more than her teacher?

Don't get your hopes up, man. Teach and be done with it.

"So tell me," he prompted. "What do you dream about?"

She sighed again and pressed her lips together. "Okay. All right. I can do this." A pause, then, "I want… God, I just want a man to touch me without the need to hurt. No, that doesn't sound right. I want to be hurt, but not in the way where the pain is given spitefully. Make sense?"

"Perfect sense. Go on."

He stared at her cheeks, growing redder by the second, and longed to stop this exercise until she was more comfortable in his company.

Evidently she already was, because she went on. "I want smacks to my arse, but not too hard, and I want several, one after the other, then some space to appreciate them, to wait until my arse stops stinging before I'm smacked again. I want to be able to suck…oh, God…suck a man without his hands clamped on my head for the purpose of him directing how I do it, how deep he goes, holding my head still so he can just ram it in until I choke. And I especially don't want to do that while being whipped so hard I bleed."

A tear trickled down her cheek.

Jesus Christ…

"I don't mind being tied up," she said, her voice brighter, "but not with anything where I can't break free. I like the illusion of being bound for good but with the reality I can tug my arms and the ties come off." She shrugged. "I don't think I want the full-on BDSM scene really, do I? My experience of it has been so…harsh that it might have put me off enjoying it now."

He understood where she was coming from. "Maybe you'll want more as time goes by. When you've started from the beginning and built trust. It's going to be difficult for you to fully let go, to embrace the pain as something pleasurable, without memories from the past making you tense and frightened."

"I know, but I feel safe with you, like I know you won't hurt me. I should be afraid of every man, but I'm not. Just of *him.*"

So this Master hadn't ruined her totally, then. She'd got away just in time. Who knew what she'd have ended up like if she'd stayed even a fortnight more? He admitted he was relieved at this latest piece of news—it made him feel less of an animal for wanting her the way he did. If she wasn't afraid of him, it would make his teachings a hell of a lot easier.

"So, are you ready to show me what you mean about sucking cock?" he asked.

She gasped, but there was no other way to put it. He may as well be blunt, continue in the way he'd always done, direct and to the point.

She nodded, fingers scrunching the fabric again before she let it go and clasped her knees. He picked up the vibrator from beside him and held it out. She felt for it, holding it by the base and raising it to chest height.

"This is so embarrassing," she said. "I don't think I can…"

"If you feel uncomfortable, then don't do it. If it helps, think of it as a real cock. Imagine you're pleasuring a man who wants nothing more than the feel of your mouth around him. He has no intention of harming you, just wants you to do what comes naturally."

Pretend you're sucking me.

She breathed in through her nose and lifted the vibrator some more until the tip rested on her bottom lip. The sight of it there, its shape and texture that of a real cock, had his dick straining in his pants. She rubbed it across her lip, and he imagined how that would feel, her soft mouth skimming the ridge of his head, breath whispering over his slit.

He squirmed and swallowed tightly.

She dashed out her tongue, then withdrew it again, as if conscious that Harry watched her every move. After another sigh, she tried it again, peeking her tongue out slower this time, licking the head in a gentle swirl from one side to the other. Christ, she was turning him on and she'd hardly done anything.

Closing her lips around the head, she pushed the vibrator into her mouth, lips stretched around the girth, gliding over the fake veins that protruded along its length. She reached halfway down and pulled back up, cheeks hollowing, then took it from her mouth, holding it between her legs. He thought for a moment she was going to lift her negligee and insert the phallus inside her, but she didn't.

Wishful thinking…

Instead, she said, "It's too hard. The vibrator, I mean. It isn't like the real thing."

"Call it what it is."

"It isn't like a real...a real cock. Do I have to use it? Can't I just show you how I like to do it on you?" She kept her eyes closed.

"Uh, I don't think that's a good idea, Ruby." *Oh, God...she's driving me crazy.*

"Don't you want me to suck you?"

"Jesus..." He sighed. "Yes, I want you to suck my dick, but darling, now isn't the right time. You're vulnerable —"

"Yes, so you keep saying, but I'll never not be vulnerable if you keep treating me as though I am. You agreed to teach me, yet you're blocking my way forward by making out I'm some scared little thing who doesn't know what she wants. Like I said just now, *he* scares me, *you* don't. I know exactly what I want, and right now it's you. So, can I suck your cock or not?"

He widened his eyes, stuck for a response.

After all, how the hell could he reply to *that*?

Chapter Seven

The only sound in the room apart from their breathing was the crackling of the fire, the delightful heat giving her, she hoped, an attractive rosy glow. For so long she'd knelt for Master, but instead of her eyes being shut by her own free will as they were now, Master had forced her to close them, covering her with darkness.

Would Harry let her suck him? She'd noticed his growing dick earlier, even though he'd tried to hide it. The way he was always so careful around her made her heart melt and her body ache with the need to feel more. Harry truly cared, and her mind couldn't move from the kiss they'd shared earlier in the chip shop. As far as she was concerned, when she went there in future she'd stand and reminisce about him and that kiss.

Will he want to keep me?

Ruby couldn't be thinking about her future in such a way. Placing the fake cock on the floor, she ran her hands over her knees, rubbing the sweat on her palms away. Would he present himself to her? For years she'd wanted to give head her way, to give her loving attention to the male organ she loved so much.

It was true what she'd said earlier. She wasn't afraid of other men, just the one man...Master.

"I'm sorry, let's forget about this," Ruby said.

Silence was a horrid weapon to use on a woman who'd been kept in the dark for so long, although she doubted Harry meant to keep her in suspense. She kept her eyes closed even as she moved to get up.

"Don't move." Harry placed a hand on her shoulder to hold her in position. He didn't squeeze down to the bone to try and make her squeal in agony. The touch was light but commanding. She enjoyed the feel of him and didn't shy away.

Taking a breath, she smiled at her own achievement and how well she knew her own body. The only man she couldn't bear to touch her was Master. Harry could touch her any way he liked.

Ruby knelt and listened.

"I'll let you suck my cock, but when I touch your cheek I want you to stop and stay still, do you understand?"

Now she shivered with delight. His voice had taken on a thick, rich timbre. He was aroused, she could hear it, but to be told what to do made her pussy pulse. The sheer panties she wore wouldn't contain much of her cream if just hearing him speak brought renewed arousal. She loved sucking cock—at least she'd loved doing it once and had even fantasised about it with Master, finding the glide of a hard staff between her wet lips intimate and amazing. To bring the man pleasure, pain, or to draw his arousal out to painstaking levels was a huge turn-on.

"Please, Harry, let me use you instead of the vibrator and show you that I can be saved. I don't want to be vulnerable for the rest of my life and I feel safe with you. I want to tell you something. Before Master..." She took a moment to swallow past the bile rising in her throat, truly hating the bastard who had taken years of her life. "Before Master, I used to work as a librarian. I'm passionate about books and reading, I love it. Anyway, after he came along, work had to stop, and then, before I knew it, so did reading. It amazes me how fast and how much I gave up for him, what he took away from me." Ruby stopped to lick her lips, heart bursting with euphoria at her bravery for finally speaking about herself. He deserved to know more after everything he'd done for her. "Thank you."

"Why are you thanking me?"

With her eyes shut she couldn't see his reaction.

"I want to show you that I'm trying to become myself again. I'm not trying to be a yes-woman just to please you. I've been the yes-woman against my will and now I want to be the woman who can say yes *and* no. Do you know what I mean?"

He didn't say a word, and Ruby was sure she'd messed up by giving some of herself, her inner thoughts. The tears that had been drying came back, a single tear escaping, trailing down her cheek. She went to wipe it away, but Harry stopped her, his hand taking hers and interlocking their fingers. A shuffle sounded before his lips touched hers — she guessed he was kneeling — and before Ruby could do anything he kissed her the same way he had in the chip shop. With full force and control.

He stopped the kiss and licked the tear from her face. "From now on with me there will be no more tears, Ruby. I want the woman you say you are, and it will give me great pleasure as a man and your Dominant to give you what you desire."

Her heart soared.

The sound of him standing again then a zipper sliding down made her gasp, the noise erotic after the romantic crackling of the fire.

"Please, can I open my eyes?"

"Why?"

"For too long I've had to keep my eyes closed and guessed what was to come. I want to see you strip away your trousers, you showing me your cock. Please, may I open them?"

"Yes, open your eyes, sweet Ruby."

Harry stood in front of her less than a foot away. She widened her eyes, didn't look up at him but watched him work his trousers. The button and zip were undone and he began to pull them down.

"May I?" she asked, reaching out to cover his hands.

She gazed up at his face and he gave her a nod, removed his hands and let her take over. Slowly, she slid them down his strong, muscled legs, noting a small dusting of hair. Extra points for wearing black boxers and not white. She hated white — Master wore them, so now they never appealed to her. The black emphasised Harry's swollen dick, snuggled in one straight line up to his hipbone.

She swallowed. Master hadn't been this big. She closed her eyes and told herself to forget about him. Harry deserved her full attention with no comparisons.

"Take my cock out, Ruby."

No second-guessing now — he had given her an order she wanted to obey. She opened her eyes again and, inch by agonising inch, peeled down his boxer shorts, revealing the tempting piece of anatomy.

With his underwear down to his thighs, his cock sprang out. She couldn't take her eyes away from him, cock long and thick, his foreskin pushed back as the length of his erection peeked out, the little slit slightly open at the top. Already pre-cum seeped out of it.

What will he taste like sliding along my tongue?

"Touch me, Ruby."

She cupped him at the base and ran her hand up to the tip and back down, resting her other on his thigh. She touched him with firm fingers and teased him with steady hands, sliding her thumb through the leaking cum and spreading the moisture all over the head. Then she raised her thumb to her lips for a taste. There was not enough to get his unique flavour, so she shuffled closer and engulfed his large head in her mouth. The contact brought a shocking wave of pleasure to her and a deep, guttural moan from the pair of them. He tasted sweet yet salty, and she went down further on him, placing her hand halfway up his erection. As she dipped her head again, her lips touched her hand. She used her fist to work the bottom half of his cock while she touched, licked and stroked his shaft with her tongue, learning everything about the shape of him.

Ruby tongued the vein down the side and followed its path to his base. She moved her hand from his leg to cup his bollocks, stopping as he touched her cheek. Her hands still on his body, she looked up at him, his fingertips remaining on her cheek. He removed it a second later and she worked him again, building up a rhythm, her hands on his cock and balls and her mouth taking him deep.

A drip of cum dropped on her tongue and she swallowed, moaning at his taste and taking more of him, right to the back of her throat. She moved her hand and mouth further down to love the parts of him she hadn't been fondling.

Harry tapped her cheek again and she stopped, taking him from her mouth. It was a test to show her who was in control.

"Touch my hair?" she asked. She wanted his hands on her hair or stroking her in some way as he exploded on her tongue.

"Are you sure?" His concern was clear.

Ruby nodded. "I know it's you. Please, Harry, just put your hands on me."

She sucked him again and his hands went to her hair. She moaned when his fingers slid through the strands. She had been so long without love and intimacy. In this brief moment she could pretend and imagine that was what they felt for each other.

He groaned and thrust his hips out gently to urge her on. She engulfed his tip then took him deep into her throat. His balls tightened, and the grip on her hair stung a little, but wasn't painful, wasn't scary. His cock pulsed and he cried out, releasing his cum. She swallowed it down, loving the taste and control he gave her. With him still stroking her hair, Ruby took everything he gave and relished the power and the play they'd just had.

He tapped her cheek for her to stop and she pulled away, her pussy soaked. Her thigh muscles were sore from kneeling, but her mind and heart were as one, at peace. The only thought that terrified her now was how easily she could be falling in love with this man. Harry had a kind heart, and she wished...a small part of her wished that with time he may come to love her a little.

If she was honest, she already believed she was in love with him. How could it be possible, though, to love a man less than twenty-four hours after meeting him and with the previous experience she'd had before?

Am I on the rebound?

"Thank you," Harry whispered, going to his knees before her and caressing her face.

Ruby didn't try to analyse the look on his face. She didn't want to be disappointed if it wasn't what she hoped it was.

"What for?" she asked.

"You gave me not only an amazing blowjob but also a piece of yourself. Librarian? I can see you in killer heels and a short skirt. I bet you drove the boys to distraction."

Ruby burst out laughing, seeing the lust on his face.

Being a librarian had been nothing like they painted in porno flicks. Far from it. She'd spent the better half of her days being around dust, cleaning and stacking the shelves. Nothing sexy in that.

"Do you need a librarian here?" she asked.

"I do own a library just off my study," he said.

The thought of him taking her and loving her while at work made her weak. "Sounds a tempting place…"

"Not as tempting as what I'm going to do to you now." His words were full of promise.

"What are you going to do to me?" she asked.

"Lie down."

Ruby studied him to try and see what he wanted to do. He smiled, reassuring her. She moved the vibrator out of her way and lay before the fire.

"Wait," she said and stood. She glanced down at him on his knees and stared into his eyes, the only light supplied by the fire.

Taking the hem of her negligee, she tugged it over her head and let it fall to the floor. Then she drew down her sheer panties, naked before him. Another big step for her—not even covering her stomach, which Master used to complain was too podgy.

Ruby took another long pull of air and lay in front of the fire, the glow making no mistake of her nudity.

"You didn't need to do that," he said.

She smiled. "I did. I wanted to. I told you, Harry— this person is who I am. No more hiding."

Never before had being naked been so liberating. She was a free woman and with Harry as a saviour she would give him everything, including her heart if he wanted it.

"You give me a great honour." He stood and followed her lead, removing his clothes and throwing them to join hers on the floor. He settled next to her.

Ruby was touched by his consideration, him allowing her to have the full heat of the fire while he lay further from it.

"I'm going to kiss you now, and love your body," Harry said. "If at any time you feel uncomfortable I want you to use your safe word. Do you remember it?"

"Butter."

"Good. You may open or close your eyes, whichever you wish. This night is for us to become acquainted with each other and then we'll develop from there."

He leaned over and kissed her. Ruby was sure she was becoming addicted to his lips, the gentle pressure and the slide of his tongue moving over her mouth trying to get her to permit him entry.

Didn't he know she'd never deny him anything?

Starting at her cheek, he caressed gently, moving the last strands of hair off her face, and trailed down to her neck, one finger gliding over her collarbone, then cupped her breast with his whole hand. He followed the path of his hand with his lips, circling the tight bud of her nipple with his tongue and sucking the hard mound in. Ruby cried out and arched into his touch, silently begging for more.

His tongue should be put away. He was deadly and wreaking havoc on her body.

Her legs shook, and she opened them wider to receive him. Harry settled between her legs, his mouth and tongue laving over the valley of her breasts, where he loved her other nipple with as much attention as the first. Nothing was painful, just sensation upon building sensation. Ruby alternated between watching him and stretching her head back every time his teeth nibbled along their sensitive route. He rained kisses over her ribcage and stomach, his tongue pressing into her belly button, making her giggle and gasp. Then he continued the journey with his lips, gliding them to her hips. He licked then laid soft kisses on the prominent bones.

Was this what it was liked to be loved?

His breath disturbed the light smattering of curls covering her mons. She loved them being stroked and touched, her hairs sparse, which she kept tidy rather than shave or wax off. She preferred to be feminine with her pubic hair. Being bare would make her feel too young.

Harry moaned and ran a light hand over her pussy. She was sensitive and wet.

"So pretty," he whispered.

He pulled her lips apart, and Ruby couldn't watch anymore—she could only give herself up to feeling. Harry exposed her clit to his view. Would she be swollen and peeking out, or would it stay hidden so he'd have to find it?

Harry licked a line from her clit to her entrance. Ruby whimpered, the contact gentle but evoking so much sensation she wasn't sure she'd be able to bear it.

"You come when I say," he said.

Ruby nodded. She wanted her pussy licked and she'd do anything he'd say to keep these emotions and sensations coming. Her pussy creamed. Her body craved the release it had long been denied. She'd take anything and everything he cared to offer.

"Open your legs wider," he commanded.

She opened her legs as wide as they would go. Harry dipped his head to look at her pussy.

"Does it look okay?" she asked, insecurity coming back.

"You're beautiful, Ruby, absolutely beautiful."

His lips showed her how much as he feasted on her.

Ruby curled her fingers into the rug. His tongue circled her clit, teasing her until she was panting and crying out for more. He gathered her juice on his fingers and eased them inside her aching channel. Ruby cried out from the invasion, her pulse hammering, his fingers stretching her. Light flicks from his tongue up and down her slit had her climax building.

She wouldn't be able to stop it.

She whimpered. It had been so long without an orgasm, and if she wasn't careful, she'd come without his permission—her first with him—creating a possible a punishment she wasn't ready to receive.

"Come for me, Ruby."

His words were a blessing. Ruby finally let go and gave herself completely to this man. He touched and loved her, his fingers fucking her cunt, his tongue dancing over her clit. She couldn't contain it any longer and screamed her completion within seconds, her eyes closed, the dance of orgasm lighting her way. She arched her back, muscles tense, the delightful, earth-shattering bliss consuming her.

His hand to her stomach brought her down slowly. He licked her juice off his fingers and laid a kiss to her pussy. Ruby knew in her heart he would always own her no matter what happened from this day forward. Already in a few short hours he had shown her how a normal relationship could be, and for that she would be forever in his debt.

Chapter Eight

Resting beside Ruby, his hand draped over her stomach, Harry cursed himself. That wasn't supposed to have happened. He'd lost all restraint when her mouth had surrounded his cock, forgotten how he'd told himself she was vulnerable and didn't need a full-on sexual relationship right now. Her explanation of it only being her Master who scared her had mollified him somewhat, but goddamn it, that wasn't the point.

His plan to show her gently and slowly how to submit had gone wrong. He should never have allowed her to suck him, because that had meant he'd had to return the pleasure.

Stop making excuses. You wanted to please her.

He stared at the ceiling, orange and yellow reflections from the fire flickering there. Last time he'd peeked at her she'd had her eyes closed, her breathing returning to normal, and although he desperately wanted to glance at her now, he stopped himself. What if he saw regret on her face? What if he saw tears?

"I'm sorry," he said. "Something happened there. I got carried away."

"I'm glad you did." She shifted onto her side and snuggled closer, fingertips trailing circles in the small of his back. "I haven't felt like that in years."

Had this Master denied her orgasms for that long? What kind of monster was he? It was clear Ruby wasn't a refined lady, but hell, Harry found he liked that. Found he wanted her to stay with him and that realisation startled him. He was used to being in control at all times, but it seemed this little waif had the ability to make him weaken. Would that work within their D/s relationship? Could he teach her when she'd already burrowed right under his skin and made him have hope for a future with her?

"It won't happen again." He continued staring at the ceiling, knowing he'd find a furrowed brow and downturned mouth if he looked at her now. It wasn't that he wanted to hurt her. Quite the opposite. He wanted to keep her safe from rushing into a new relationship when she still had issues from the last. Or could he heal her as he loved her? He wasn't sure.

"Why not?" she asked, voice small and barely there.

"I..." He sighed. "I feel I took advantage of you, even though you wanted it."

"Fuck, yeah, I wanted it." She propped herself up on one elbow. "And I want it again. More. Different things. I want you."

She didn't sound needy or desperate. On the contrary, she was resolute, her words spoken by a woman who knew her own mind and feelings. Still, he wasn't comfortable with having tasted her, having jumped a few levels of teaching to get straight down to the sexual pleasure side of it. He should have refused her request to swallow his cock.

He turned his head and took in the sight of her. No frown. No downturned mouth. Instead, she gave him a smile, and her eyes were alight with life, something he would never have expected to see when she'd arrived. He remembered how those eyes had looked as she'd stared at the kitchen door, the fear swirling there, the deep crevice between her eyebrows. She had been frightened then, but now she was a different person. He'd like to think he had a hand in that, but maybe the knowledge that she was safe here was what had made the change in her.

"This has all happened rather quickly," he said, lifting a hand to stroke her cheek with the backs of his fingers. "I'm concerned you're not really ready for this, that I've crossed the line between teacher and student."

"But this kind of teacher-student relationship involves sex, so what's the problem?" She raised her hand to grasp his wrist then planted a kiss on his palm. "I'm the happiest I've been in *years,* Harry. The safest. Do you realise how that makes me feel? Shit, I want to dance, to laugh until my ribs hurt, to run out there and shout at the sky that I'm free and everything's fucking wonderful."

She got up and twirled in a circle, arms swinging, her features so relaxed she appeared young and carefree. The sight of her ribs sticking out and some old and recent scars marring her skin made him want to get up and take her in his arms, smooth the scars into non-existence and feed her until that bird-cage look to her torso disappeared.

Time. He needed lots of it.

She span, arms out at her sides. "Can you feel it, Harry? Feel how bloody wonderful everything is?"

He sat up and watched her, and yes, he felt it. It oozed from her, infusing him, and a chuckle brewed in his chest. She laughed — eyes closed, hair swaying — and pranced about the room. Her mood was infectious, and he couldn't resist rising. He went to her, stopping her dance to hold her close. She rested her cheek against his chest, and he weaved his fingers through her hair, grasping it tight in his fist. He tugged gently until she looked up at him.

"Are you ready for what we originally set out to do?" He tightened his grip.

"Yes."

He kissed the tip of her nose — couldn't resist it — and released her hair at the same time as gently pushing her away.

"Kneel in front of the settee," he instructed. "Belly flat on the seat. Hold your hands at the bottom of your back and wait for me to return."

She nodded, and rather than admonish her for not saying '*Yes, Sir*,' he walked into the hallway then pounded the stairs to reach his bedroom. There, he opened a large wooden chest at the foot of his bed and selected a small paddle. Oh, he knew she hadn't liked them before, but he had to show her how it *should* be used. After selecting a bottle of massage oil, he went downstairs and stood in the living room doorway.

She looked beautiful in the pose he'd directed, her buttocks rounded and slightly spread, her fingers entwined. She faced away from him, and her hair spilled across her back and draped over her shoulders, some ends resting on the leather. He frowned at the faint stripes on her back — administered with a cruel whip, he had no doubt — and sighed inwardly at the abuse she'd suffered. Why had her Master been so cruel? From what he could tell, Ruby was an exceptional, lovely woman who inspired nothing in him but the need to care for her. The previous man in her life had been a fool, controlling her so much he'd snuffed out the magical essence that was Ruby — the one thing that made her so delightful to Harry.

He held the paddle behind his back and walked towards her. She didn't tense — something he'd expected to be a habit — and he was inordinately pleased about that. She trusted him already, that much was clear, and the niggling doubt came again that perhaps she trusted him too much.

It wouldn't just hurt *him* when he set her free.

"Shift your feet together," he said, then knelt, one knee either side of her calves.

He placed the paddle on the floor and tapped the handle so the toy was out of sight beneath the sofa. Opening the massage oil, he poured some into his cupped hand, stood the bottle on the floor, then spread the fluid over his palms to warm it.

"Keep your safe word in mind. We'll be testing your pain levels and what you find acceptable. You must *not* take more pain than you can handle. I want you to be honest and let me know when it's no longer giving you pleasure. You'll please me by doing this. Do you understand?"

She nodded, eyes closed, and a lock of hair fell to cover them.

"I'm going to begin."

He waited for her to tense, for her muscles to bunch in her anticipation of him striking her, but she remained plaint, comfortable.

Good.

Scooting back to give himself more room, Harry pressed his hands to her ass cheeks. She didn't flinch, so he smoothed the skin, wanting to ready it for the paddle. He spent some time caressing, then slid his hands between her arse cleft, instantly admonishing himself for it. But that dark, shadowy crack lured him, held so much promise that he was unable to hold back. Going against his rules, he moved one hand lower and cupped her mound, the heat from her slit warming his palm. If he just inched his hand a little further back, he'd touch her clit…

No. Stop it.

She whimpered and he withdrew, once again massaging her arse.

"Don't stop," she whispered. "Put your hand back there. Please. Sir…"

"No."

Control surged inside him, and he reached down for the paddle. Moving so he knelt to one side of her legs, he judged the amount of swing room he had. Not much, but he didn't need it. Short, sharp smacks were what he was after. He raised the paddle and brought it down slowly, connecting with her right buttock with hardly any force. She jerked but still appeared relaxed, and he guessed her soft gasp was more from not expecting the strike than any pain. From what she'd told him, she was used to so much worse.

He hit her again, harder this time, and waited for a negative reaction. None came, so he created a pattern of striking, each one harder than the last. At the point he thought she'd buckle, when the hit made her ass bloom red, she jutted her bottom out for more. He obliged, giving her three whacks in quick succession, pleased to hear another whimper coming from beneath that curtain of hair. Spurred on, he smacked some more, his cock stiffening as he took in the sight of her arse cheeks burning. She had to be on the border between pleasure and pain now, so the final hits should tell him her threshold.

After three harder connections, she unclasped her hands and held one up.

"Have you had enough?" he asked. "If so, use your safe word."

"No, Sir, I...I just need a minute."

He'd found her level, where she was starting to feel uncomfortable, and he wasn't happy at continuing. He knew she'd have mastered the art of switching her mind off, and he'd be damned if he'd allow that to happen with him.

"Be honest," he said. "I'll be disappointed if you're not. I'll ask you again. Have you had enough?"

"Yes, Sir," she whispered.

"Good girl. Now, what do you think I used on you?"

She lowered her hand to the settee and fiddled with her hair. "A bit of wood? Like a thin plank? It felt wooden anyway."

"Get up and look at me."

She pushed off the seat and turned her face towards him. He held up the paddle, and she widened her eyes, one hand rising to cover her mouth.

"You used *that*?" she asked, her voice muffled.

"I did. And it wasn't so bad, was it?"

She shook her head, staring at the paddle with confusion in her eyes.

"It isn't the implement that is wrong but how it's used," he said, keeping his tone low. "I can guarantee that any toy used by me in our play will not hurt anywhere near how it did with your previous Master. Do you trust me to use a whip next time?"

She nodded again, although a snippet of fear lingered on her face.

"I promise I won't *ever* go beyond your comfort level, Ruby."

"Okay."

She lowered her hand, a picture of vulnerability before him—her hair tousled, her generous breasts lifting and falling with each breath she took. He couldn't deny her reassurance and reached out, nestling her body against his.

"It'll all work out," he murmured into her hair. "I'll fix you, then you can go out there knowing what's acceptable and what isn't. No one will ever hurt you again because you'll understand who is a genuine Dom and who is in it for cruelty."

I don't want you to go out there and find someone else...

"How long will it take, Harry? Your lessons, I mean."

"A couple of weeks, perhaps a bit longer. It depends how we get on."

"Then I'll hope for two weeks or more," she whispered. "I like it here. Like you." She raised her head and looked at him. "You saved me, d'you know that?"

Embarrassed under such sincere scrutiny, he blushed and cupped her cheek. "I rather think you saved me."

"What d'you mean?"

He stroked her cheek with his thumb. "Nothing. I shouldn't have said anything. Now, I think it's time we washed off that massage oil and I applied some salve. I wouldn't want you getting sore."

"Salve? Is that what you're meant to do?" She frowned.

"Some use it, some don't. I prefer to know my subs are well cared for. Come along. I'll sort you out and then it's bed for you. We have a long day of lessons ahead tomorrow."

* * * *

Harry lay in bed listening to the house creaking. It was as though the old building had a voice, that it grumbled as it settled for the night, groaning about having to withstand the harsh weather. He smiled at his silly thoughts and brought Ruby to mind instead. She probably thought the lessons coming her way were sexual, but she had a lot to learn about herself before he could press her with more spankings. What he had in mind was a simple day of allowing her to move about the house freely so she could understand that being tied up for hours on end wasn't a requirement of all Doms.

Sunday promised to be an interesting study.

He thought about her spanking then, how she'd reacted so well, yet her thinking he'd used a plank of wood and letting him spank her regardless was somewhat disturbing. Perhaps she'd been struck with such an implement before and she thought every Dom used one? There was so much she had yet to tell him, but he wouldn't push. The memories were perhaps better left unexplored for the rest of the weekend. God knew she could do with respite from them.

How was she faring now, alone in her room? He strained for sounds from above—he'd chosen that room so he could hear her moving about, the loose floorboard by the door ideal for alerting him that she had left the room—but heard nothing out of the ordinary. He worried that despite her telling him she'd be fine as she began walking up the stairs, the memories of what she'd endured before would visit her as nightmares. She'd managed very well in appearing to combat them during the evening, but her sometimes panicked glances behind her in the shopping centre were more than enough proof she would take a long time to heal.

If she woke in fear, he'd be there. She knew where his room was, he'd made a point of showing her just before they retired, and he'd also let her know that if she needed him, not to hesitate in seeking him out.

As if his thoughts of Ruby made her get out of bed, Harry listened to her soft footsteps then the jarring creak of the floorboards. He forced himself to remain in position. She had to come to him, to learn to take matters into her own hands, instead of him rushing from his room to seek her out and ask what was wrong. Yes, she needed that kind of caring behaviour from a Dom, too, but for now he wanted to build up her confidence, let her see she could make decisions without being reprimanded for it.

It wasn't long before a soft knock came and his door inched open. Her face appeared, her peeking around the frame, and he smiled at her.

"I can't sleep," she said. "Can I...?"

Of course she bloody can.

"If that's what makes you happy, yes," he said.

She came in, closed the door, and snuggled in bed beside him. He held her close, smiling as in no time at all her breathing evened out and a soft snore huffed from her lips.

If he wasn't careful he could get used to this.

Damn.

* * * *

Master couldn't sleep. For the second night in a row rest eluded him, and he paced his living room, scoring double tracks in the fluffy cream rug. He should have been tired from erecting his contraption at the club—a donation, he'd said, to the place that had allowed him to meet people of like mind. The owner had eyed him with suspicion, but really, what was the harm in him contributing a new thing to play with?

In any case, he didn't care what the owner thought. She'd accepted the donation, leaving him to set it up on the wall in one of the empty play rooms, and he'd spent the time forming the plan that had sprouted when he'd seen Margaret with Knowles.

He only hoped it would work to his advantage.

Sunday evenings saw Dominants and subs gathering at the club for their weekly meeting. Not everyone attended—some preferred to come and play every so often, keeping their private lives just that— but many used it as an opportunity to swap stories and spend time in the company of people who had the same predilections. Knowles was one of them. As far as Master could remember, Knowles had never missed a meeting, but now he had Margaret perhaps the man would refrain from attending.

He hasn't in the past when he's been teaching subs.

But what if he wasn't just teaching? What if, as he suspected, Knowles and Margaret were a proper couple?

He cursed, thumping his thigh as a surge of anger burst inside him. That bitch had planned this. Met Knowles somehow and waited for the right time to run to him. Master hadn't removed her collar, hadn't given her permission to leave, so the chit had a cheek in thinking she had gained her liberty. Oh, he knew full well she probably thought she had the right to leave him whenever she chose, but as far as he was concerned, she should have obeyed his rules, not the lax, too-giving ones most other Doms and subs played by.

"She belongs to me until I choose to let her go."

Master glanced at the clock. It was close to midnight and, despite the snow, he was ready to go out and put the next part of his plan into action. Shrugging on his coat, he left the house and drove off towards the countryside. The roads were treacherous the further he got from Manchester, but they weren't so bad that he'd end up stranded. After all, no fresh snow had fallen for two days, and Knowles would have used this road to take Margaret shopping, so it wouldn't be that bad.

He grimaced at the thought of his sub travelling these roads with that man.

He parked on the verge beside the entrance to Knowles' property, his vehicle hidden by high hedges. The last thing he needed was for Knowles to hear him coming up the driveway. No, he wanted anonymity for what he was about to do, so that Knowles would definitely take Margaret to the club Sunday night. For all Master knew, Margaret had told her new Dom all about him. Yes, it was best Master remain incognito.

He tromped up the driveway, walking in a rut created by Knowles' tyres, the packed-down snow slippery. Although Master wore gloves, his fingers were still cold, so he shoved his hands in his pockets.

At the house, he stared up at the impressive façade, nodding at the realisation of why Ruby had chosen Knowles. She'd gone with Master for his money, he was sure of it, and with Knowles having so much more, it stood to reason she'd find the lenient Dom a better prospect.

Master could only hope the teachings he'd instilled in her would win out in the end and he'd have her chained up in his house with no chance of running ever again.

He peered through a window beside the front door. The curtains hadn't been drawn, which enabled him to spot a fire dying in the grate, the orange embers glowing, making him wish he sat before it. Yes, he could see himself living in a place like this.

His hate for Knowles grew further.

Reaching into his inside jacket pocket, he pulled out the six-by-six card he'd printed himself, quite impressed with how authentic it looked. He took the steps to the front door and slid the card through the letterbox, satisfied when a soft whisper of sound told him it had floated to the floor.

He nodded—a curt, one-dip-of-the-head action—and turned to face the road. He couldn't see his Land Rover from here and suspected if Knowles was a light sleeper and heard the letterbox open, the man wouldn't see it either if he looked out of an upstairs window.

Happy with how things were going, Master walked back down the driveway and got into his car, starting the engine and wincing at how loud it seemed out here in the sticks. No matter, there was nothing he could do about it now.

He drove home, congratulating himself on a job well done.

Tomorrow night he would see Margaret again.

Tomorrow night she'd wish she'd never been born.

Chapter Nine

Something brushed along Ruby's cheek then down her neck. She moaned, batting at whatever caused her discomfort. She turned over in bed, mumbling. The stroking continued.

"All right, all right, I'm awake," she grumbled and looked up into Harry's beautiful eyes.

He sat on the end of the bed holding out a feather. "I couldn't resist."

"Is that how you wake up all your women?"

"No, usually I go for a little spanking session before shower sex," he said, eyes sparkling. "Kidding. I came to see if you were hungry for some breakfast."

Ruby smiled and her heart melted. He was the sweetest man she'd ever met. She lifted the blanket to her chin and waited for him to continue stroking and talking.

She frowned when he didn't.

"What's the matter?" he asked.

"I'm waiting for you to tell me what else we're doing today."

Master had always given her a list of what he hoped to accomplish and how he planned to dish out punishments. He even had a punishment scale of one to ten. She shuddered, remembering what happened to her when her star ended up on the naughty cloud.

Last night had been a revelation to her. Being spanked with a paddle then soothed with salve. Master used to slap so hard the pain crashed through her entire body, leaving her in no doubt of the pain he could cause with an implement. She would then be expected to get on all fours while he fucked her hard and rough, even though her arse was on fire and the welts almost bleeding. Master expected her to clean up her mess—if she was weak enough to bleed then she could clean up her own weakness.

"Hey, come back to me," Harry said softly, holding her cheeks.

"You really are a special man," she told him.

In her experience, no man ever cared about the woman they'd fucked. Last night, after sucking him off, she'd waited for him to leave her wanting as all other men she'd been with had. But he'd licked her and brought her to climax, knocking every other notion out of the water.

"I'm just a man like every other."

"No, you're not."

Harry didn't know how special he was. Ruby was going to be the one to show him how much.

He pulled away. "Do you like eggs and bacon?"

"A full English?"

How long had it been since she'd had so much food on one plate? Fried eggs, crispy bacon… What about a fried slice? She let the blanket drop and touched her small stomach. Was she still too fat? She pulled at the skin, shocked to see she struggled to get a firm grip on her own flesh.

"What are you doing, Ruby? Stop it." He reached over and stopped her from hurting herself.

"Am I fat?" she asked, her heart breaking inside, the last straps of Master's punishment still holding her firmly in place, it seemed.

Her weight had always fluctuated. Since Master had limited her food intake the pounds had fallen off, but she'd spent most of the time starving or feeling sick if she ate too much. Like yesterday when they'd eaten fish and chips. The food had been amazing—greasy and everything she'd craved—but soon after she'd had the desire to go and throw everything back up.

"Look at me, Ruby," Harry demanded, forcing her with a hand on her chin to stare back. "You're not fat and it will give me great pleasure to feed you."

A tear settled in the corner of her eye, and he moved to catch it, but she pulled back to wipe it herself. How many times would she cry before she started to make noise? Every time she took a step forward she suddenly took two steps back. Here she was being a fucking cry baby again.

She smiled at him. "Yes, I'd love a full English."

Would she be able to keep it down? Ruby gasped as Harry placed a hand over her concave stomach. His hand curved with it and she wondered what he was thinking. Did he find her repulsive? What would he think if he saw a picture of her prior to Master's influence? She hadn't been overweight but she'd been a lot more rounded with flesh on her bones rather than the protruding points now sticking out of her skin.

Harry leant down and kissed her on the forehead, pushing back strands of hair. "You're a really beautiful woman and you should never think differently."

"Would you like me with a little more meat on my bones?"

"Ruby, I'll like you whatever way you come. It's you here that I like." He pressed a hand to her chest, over her heart.

Harry really knew how to say the nicest things to a girl. She covered his hand and brought it to her lips, laying kisses along his knuckles.

"Thank you."

Harry looked at her for a while in silence. He seemed to want to say more but in the end he got up, extracted his hand and moved towards the door. He turned to look at her. "Until you're ready to go, this is your home."

As a parting shot it was powerful, but it reminded Ruby their time together would eventually come to an end, and she didn't know if she'd be ready for it. After he left, she spent time getting washed and ready before going to her own room to pick an outfit they'd chosen together the previous day. Mini-skirts and short, tight tank tops were pushed aside. She wasn't ready for them yet, but she could use the excuse of the cold to allow her to wrap up warm. Eventually, she decided on a pair of loose-fitting trousers—she'd need the room after her first full breakfast in years—and a plain white blouse. Her underwear was a simple cotton set.

Before leaving the comfort of her bedroom, she took the time to look in the mirror. Her reflection shocked her. The outfit highlighted her weight loss dramatically.

Ruby began to wonder why Master had picked her up at the library all those years ago if he would only ever be disappointed with her and want to change every single aspect of who she was as a person. To a point, she understood why he would want to change her attitude and the way she talked. Compared to a lot of people in the posh parts, she was rough-sounding, and to some even vulgar, but why would he stick it out torturing her to make her someone she clearly wasn't? She'd noticed Harry wincing at some of her words and the way she talked. Did he find her offensive?

Shaking her head against the horrid thoughts, she quickly ran a brush through her hair and left the room following the delicious scent of eggs and bacon. Her tummy rumbled as the smell grew stronger, and she found him doing a flip-toss with some mushrooms in a pan. Harry turned when she entered, gesturing for her to sit at a place setting. A cup of coffee already awaited her. Cringing, she gingerly took a sip then smiled when she put the cup down. Bless him, he'd gone and brought her some cheap shit.

If he cared so much to make this extra effort, why did he want her gone in a couple of weeks? Ruby played with the fork on her mat and watched him work the stove. His fine arse called to her. Tight and firm. She imagined sinking her nails into the flesh as he rode her hard and fast, forcing her to take all of his huge cock. A blush heated her cheeks, and she attempted to cover it with her hands. Embarrassing to be caught ogling and fantasising about the man who'd come out into the cold to rescue you.

Several minutes later, he came over with two plates, each with a generous serving of bacon, mushrooms, sausages, fried eggs and beans, all finished off with crispy toast.

"Sorry, I didn't get round to doing the fried slice," he said.

Ruby laughed. After this treasure trove on her plate she'd be lucky to walk afterwards.

Harry pulled a newspaper and a card across the table and began to read.

Ruby ate her breakfast, forcing herself not to be nosy and not to see what he had. But she couldn't resist asking, "Anything interesting in the paper?" Everything about the man who was fast becoming her ultimate crush intrigued her. He was far better than the Edward Cullens of this world. At least this guy was freaking real and she stood a chance of being fucked by him.

Would he go and watch the new *Twilight* movie with her? With Master, she'd been controlled to the degree he even monitored what she watched.

This is ridiculous, thinking about him. Stop being so bloody negative. Master is gone and not coming back into my life. Ever!

Harry cleared his throat. "Just the usual chaos and tragedy that is the norm these days in our small country." He sighed, pushing the newspaper to one side. He picked up the card, piercing a mushroom at the same time.

"I take it everything is bad news," she said.

"If you count the crime and unemployment, then yes. If you count me sitting here enjoying my breakfast with a beautiful woman at my side, then no."

Ruby could purr with all of his compliments. Harry frowned, turning the card over, then put it further away from them at the corner of the table. He ate his food without any further expression.

"What's the matter?" she asked.

"Nothing, nothing."

"You said 'nothing' twice, which usually means something's wrong. Please tell me."

She reached out and placed a comforting hand on his arm. He moaned and gave in, handing her the card. Ruby didn't understand. It was a message about a Master-and-sub meeting. She flipped the card over to see if there were any more clues, but a black design covered the back.

"What is it?" she asked.

"Nothing to concern yourself with."

"Is this the club you attend as a…a Master?" Ruby had heard of such meetings, but after being with her own Master, she'd never believed they really happened, let alone had men like Harry attending.

"Yes, a group of professional Masters get together at an exclusive club to talk and train new subs, among other things," he said, drinking his cup of horse shit.

"You're going tonight?"

"I go every Sunday but I think I'll give it a miss tonight."

They continued to eat in silence. The imposing card hogged all Ruby's attention. Was it a sign for her to go with him? To take the next step and trust him with her body and mind out in the public eye? Among strangers who lived the lifestyle?

When her stomach pretty much complained it was full, Ruby put her plate away from her and picked up the card, twirling it in her fingers while waiting for Harry to finish eating. The corners dug into her skin, and the gold-embossed fancy writing continued to catch her eye.

Finally, after what felt like a lifetime, Harry finished and made to clear the table. Dropping the card, she took over.

"I'll do the dishes." She took their plates and moved to the sink already filled with bubbles.

"You don't have to clean for me, Ruby, you're my guest," Harry pointed out.

She ignored him, wanting to do something to digest her crazy thoughts about going to that meeting. He finished his coffee while she pondered the possibilities of visiting the club and being part of his world outside this house. She cleaned all of the grease and muck off the pots, then dried and cleaned the work surfaces. Master's training had turned her into an efficient beast.

Using a fresh cup, she poured Harry more horse sh—coffee. She placed it on the table.

He was flicking through the newspaper again.

"Thanks, Ruby."

She wrung her hands. How did she ask if she could go with him?

"What's the matter, Ruby?" He put the newspaper down and moved his chair so he faced her. Opening his legs to make room, he caught her hands and brought her between his spread thighs. He closed them, trapping her close to his body—a simple contact of his legs that sent shock waves of heat rolling up to her pussy. Biting her lip to keep from moaning, she turned her eyes away.

"When you're with me, show me how I affect you," he said. "I can see you containing a moan and I want to hear you express it. Show me what I do to you."

Ruby shook her head, and the devil placed his hands on her thighs. As they travelled up her body, the heat of him warmed through the thin fabric of her trousers. She moaned, no longer able to contain the sound. He let go of her, clearly satisfied.

"Now, what can I do for you, young lady? What do you want to ask that had you wringing your hands?"

"I don't want you to miss your meeting." *That was a good start.*

"One week won't hurt, and I have you to keep me company."

His fingers locked with hers and he smiled, melting even more than her heart this time.

"What if I was to come with you?" Biting her lip again, she looked down, not wanting to see his reaction in case he was disgusted by her idea.

His finger under her chin lifted her gaze to his.

"I don't think you're ready for that bit, honey."

"I won't do anything. Just keep you company. That way I won't feel like a total pain for stopping you going. And I can watch. Learn."

Harry shook his head and leant back. On instinct, Ruby wrapped her hands round his neck, tugging the strands of hair at the base of his skull. She held his face, forcing him to look at her. When he reared back again and a gasp escaped his lips, and no backlash of punishment came, she didn't know what to do. His lips beckoned to her, and before she could stop herself she covered those lips with her own. The moment they connected, the electricity around them spiked. Her nipples pulsed as a fresh wave of heat rushed through her. He cupped behind her neck with one hand grasping her hair and pulled the long strands, easing her away from him. She let go and gave herself over to her new Master. He stood, towering over her, but she didn't feel threatened. Instead, she was extremely turned on by his dominant move.

He was taller, stronger and more powerful than her, and his act of transferring power to get her to submit to him was clear.

"You would never be a pain or problem to me, Ruby. Never."

He stroked a finger along her cheek and she closed her eyes. The touch was gentle, his words poetic. "Please let me go with you?"

"Why do you want to go?" he asked.

"So I can see other people in the lifestyle. It'll help me to know it's not only you who's kind and generous. Help me see you're not the only Master who allows his women free rein to speak their minds and to be submissive to your needs without ever taking mine away."

"Why else do you want to go?"

"I want to prove to you I can be your sub."

With that admittance, Ruby knew with all of her heart she had no desire to leave Harry's side. They'd known each other such a short time, but some of the great love stories had taken a matter of moments. Love did exist. She'd seen it in people before Master had taken her away, clear with her own eyes.

Harry shook his head and turned away, picking up the card and newspaper. "I don't think you're ready, but if *you* think you are and you trust me, then you'd better get some clothes ready for tonight. Hang them up, give them time to air out."

Ruby jumped on the spot, happy to be going with him, owned and claimed by Harry. She twirled in a circle and clapped her hands, going giddy.

"What shall I do after that?" she asked, still doing her merry dance.

"Explore the house. Have fun."

Ruby started off walking up the stairs until her excitement got the better of her and she ran. The freedom and chance to investigate brought a new lease of life. She danced in circles once she reached the top floor, then ran back downstairs to the first. The handrails were designed like those in the movies that children slid down. Unable to resist, she cocked a leg over the side and once she was comfortable, let go, sliding down to the ground floor. Landing on her feet, she went back to do it again. Four more times she repeated the slide, her giggles echoing off the walls.

"What the bloody hell are you doing?" Harry came out of the kitchen in time to see her making the journey again.

"Having fun like you told me to. Come on, give it a try." She took his hand and led him up the stairs.

He tried to pull out of her grip.

"Come on!" she growled, tugging him along.

"This is childish."

"But fun."

"Ruby!"

Hands on hips, she glared at him. "You told me to have fun and finally I listen and now you're...what? Going to tell me to stop?"

"No, of course not."

"Then give it a try. It's *fun*."

Urging him towards the rail, she raised her eyebrows and waited.

He glared at her, cheeks stained pink. He sighed. "Fine. I'll do it this once."

Harry went down, landing perfectly. Ruby hooted. They took it in turns until finally they collapsed in a heap on the floor, laughing.

Ruby laid her head on his stomach. "Told you it was fun."

He stroked her hair and chuckled, the movement making her head bounce. "I suppose I'd better listen to you more often."

"Yes, you should."

* * * *

Some time later, Harry took her by the hand and led her through every room of the house.

"What about the work you were doing in your office?" she asked.

"I work all the time and it'll still be there when I get back."

Ruby smiled, seeing a whole new playful side to Harry. Going down the handrail seemed to have invited the child inside him out and in doing so changed the atmosphere between them again.

They went to the living room and she recalled them exploring one another last night, her arse finally properly introduced to the paddle. He pointed out certain features and his art. She found he even had a swimming pool.

"You had this and you didn't tell me?" she said.

"I was saving it for a nice surprise."

After the tour, they landed in his library.

"Now, I don't think this is going to be as big as some of the libraries out there, but it could get you back into the swing of things," he said, showing her one of the most expensive and rare collections of books she'd ever seen.

Display pages of classics along with modern texts adorned each wall in spaces between shelves.

"Where did you get all these from?" She moved to a shelf and inspected the collection of horror books before moving down to see first editions.

"Passed down from generation to generation, and so my children will get these books, but with all the e-readers out these days, I don't think they'll be too thrilled with my collection," he joked.

"I know what you mean. But there's nothing like the smell of a book, new or old. I love holding them in my hands." Ruby pulled one off the shelf and opened it, smiling at the dedication. She loved reading those. It made the book more personal and memorable.

"Yes, I can see you like that," he said.

She brought the book to her nose and smelt the musty old cover. Fun and happy memories assailed her from when she'd worked as a librarian. "The worst mistake throughout my whole life was giving up my job and going with *him*. Most young women would probably hate being stuck in some boring old library cataloguing books and placing them back on the shelves, but I loved it."

"You can use this place as your own personal library if you want."

"Do you mean that?"

"I wouldn't have said it if I didn't."

Giggling, she replaced the book then charged at him. She jumped, and he caught her, his arms about her back, her legs circling his waist.

"I knew you'd catch me," she said, breathless.

"Always."

She smiled and brushed her lips against his. She could lose herself in his kiss. The touch and taste of him was exotic and unlike anything she was used to. Harry gave pleasure and made sure she took as much as he did from the moment.

Without thinking, she pulled away and pressed her nose into the curve of his neck.

"I think I'm in love with you," she whispered.

She didn't know if he'd heard her, but if he did, he gave no indication—no change in his stance, no faster breathing. He held her against him until the clock chimed in the hallway, signalling their daytime was coming to an end.

Harry let her go, stroking her cheek. "It's time to get ready."

Her heart fell at still receiving no reciprocating response, but she wanted nothing more than to be the perfect sub to him. Smiling, she took his hand and followed him out of the library, giving the books a last, lingering look.

It felt like her life was only just beginning, and for the first time in what seemed forever, she was happy to live it.

Chapter Ten

With Ruby's arm curled around his, her hand on his wrist, Harry led her through the club doorway and into the elegant foyer. The usual receptionist, Veronica, a brunette in her forties who would have looked at home in a lawyer's office, greeted them with a smile and raised eyebrows over her red spectacles, an action he knew was specifically for him. He trained subs from here, never from outside, and her speculation amused him. Harry Knowles breaking from the norm? Unheard of.

Well, people will have to get over it.

He produced the card from his suit jacket pocket, conscious of Ruby shaking — from nerves or excitement, he wasn't sure. Whatever it was, he squeezed her arm against his body with his and gave her a brief smile. She beamed back at him — it was excitement, then — and her eyes sparkled.

She looked beautiful tonight, her short black dress emphasising her slight body, the high black heels seeming to extend her legs. They appeared to go on forever, and damn, if they weren't here, he'd…

He ignored his thoughts and placed the card on the faux oak desk, smiling at Veronica. She frowned and slid it towards her—reading, her lips moving with every word.

"Uh, where did you get this?" she asked, turning it over and eyeing the black pattern on the back then looking up at him.

"It must have been posted late last night." Harry frowned. "Is there a problem?"

Veronica shrugged. "Only that I haven't seen one of these yet tonight and I wasn't aware there was any special meeting just because of a new piece of play equipment." She shrugged. "Always the last to know these things. Anyway, you know the rules, so here you go."

She pushed a guest book across the desk, and Harry signed them in. He felt for Veronica not being told about this. On special occasions she dressed up in full bondage gear, loving the chance to express herself. Tonight's outfit of a black pencil skirt and white blouse probably made her feel just what she was—a receptionist.

Harry nodded to her and led Ruby to a door at the rear. Once through it and in a long hallway with several mahogany doors either side, he stopped and curved his hands around the tops of her arms.

"Nervous?" he asked.

"Yes, and excited. This is nothing like I expected. It looks like a bloody doctor's surgery." She indicated the doors with a dip of her head. "There's all the consulting rooms, look, and back there's where you sit and wait for your appointment. Except my doctor's place doesn't have leather chairs and sofas and those beautiful potted palms."

He chuckled. "Well, through that door at the end is where everything is a little different. These are some of the play rooms, dungeons, the more private ones for one-on-one interaction. Through there" — he jerked his thumb in the direction of the hallway's end — "is the meeting room, and from there you can take the stairs and go into the more adventurous dungeons." He stroked her face, loving the wonder clearly written there.

"More adventurous?" She widened her eyes.

"Yes, as in…well, some rooms look like torture chambers to the untrained eye, but of course, they're not. I'll show you once the meeting is over, if you like."

"All right. And…will you do anything to me while we're in them?" She smiled conspiratorially, a glint of hope in her eyes.

"That depends how comfortable you are after you've seen the show."

"There'll be a show?" She frowned.

"Yes, there's usually a weekly show every Sunday where a new sub is presented, or a Dom and sub wish to provide entertainment or share what they've learned."

"Oh my God. And we'd watch them…*doing* things?"

He grinned, stomach bunching at his thoughts of watching Ruby observing them. "Oh, yes, we'd watch. Are you happy with that?"

She blinked several times as she processed the information. "Um, I don't know. I think so. Oh, hang on. I'm not sure… It seems a bit rude."

"You could try it, and if it isn't your thing we can leave. It isn't a problem, Ruby. You must do whatever makes you feel right. I will never make you do otherwise, do you understand?" He raised a hand and brushed her cheek, the feel of her soft skin stirring his cock to life. Inwardly he cursed. Walking into the meeting room with a hard-on wasn't his style. Once in there when the show began, yes, it was difficult to suppress it, but not now.

"Okay," she said, nodding, as though convincing herself it would be all right.

"I mean it," he said. "Do *not* do anything just to please me. It has to be for yourself first. What makes you happy makes me happy. Understand?"

Her eyes watered, and he pulled her close, one hand at the small of her back, the other in her hair. He pressed her cheek to his chest and smiled when she snaked her arms around him.

"You're too good to me, Harry."

"No," he said, caressing her hair. "I'm not good enough." *Because I want to keep you, never set you free to explore with other Doms. I want to love you.*

Hell, she was under his skin, beneath the muscles, right in his goddamn marrow.

"You'll never know…" She eased her head back and looked up at him. "I…I'm so glad I ended up at your place."

"You never did explain just how you got there. It's quite a way on foot from the city."

She bit her lip. "I hitched, planned to get far away, but the guy —"

"You got in a car with a *man?*" He clamped his jaw closed, fighting the urge to shout. "My God, Ruby! Don't ever do that again!"

You won't have to if you stay with me.

"I won't. I'm sorry, but you don't realise how bad it was, how much I needed to get away. I was trying to get to my mother's. He, the guy, thought I was a prostitute and he—"

"Jesus Christ... Where does your mother live?"

"A few miles from you, but thinking about it now, it would have been a shock for her if I'd just turned up. She... I haven't seen her since..."

Her eyes watered again, and he crushed her to him.

"We'll talk about this another time. You can ring her, and I'll take you to see her once the weather improves, all right?"

She nodded against his chest, and he gently pushed her back to look into her eyes.

"We'll get through this, understand?"

She smiled and blew out a shaky breath. "I understand...Sir."

A cheeky smile lit up her face, and his insides melted.

Damn. How will I ever manage without her?

"Come," he said brusquely, cursing himself for sounding so terse. "We'll be late for the start of the meeting."

He held out his arm for Ruby to grasp and led her through the end doorway, his thoughts in turmoil. He'd begun to care for her more than he'd thought possible. Her revelation of how she'd arrived at his home that night swirled in his mind, making him think of what could have happened if the driver hadn't let her out of the car. So he didn't torture himself further with macabre visions, he glanced around the meeting room for sight of someone he knew. Rows of black leather bucket chairs were in front of the stage, a polished-wood, the podium set front and centre. Several of his friends and their subs stood before it. Others chattered in small groups, while some had paired off, deep in conversation.

"I'm going to introduce you to my friends," he said, guiding her towards them, seeing Judge Leo Jones had no partner tonight. "They're very nice, so no need to be nervous."

He glanced at her and she nodded, staring up at him as though he was some kind of god. He'd have to watch she didn't become too attached. Her telling him earlier that she loved him... Well, it had shocked him to the degree he couldn't respond. She was suffering on the rebound, he knew that. No way did she love him in the real sense.

Did she?

He wasn't sure now, what with the look on her face saying otherwise. She trusted him, that much was clear, and it seemed while she was at his side she was a beautiful, tiny butterfly just freed from her cocoon, content to settle on his arm for now.

But butterflies fly away and discover other things, places, people...

"Harry, old boy! Damn good to see you."

Leo's loud greeting gained the attention of others in the room, and those with him turned to watch Harry and Ruby approach.

"I see you've brought a guest." Leo nodded his salt-and-pepper-covered head once and held out his hand. "Pleased to meet you...?"

"Ruby," she said quietly, allowing him to shake her hand.

"Ruby. Lovely. Sub name or real?" He quirked a fuzzy eyebrow.

"Real," she said.

Harry smiled, pleased she'd answered and didn't act so subservient that she waited for him to do it for her or to give permission. Other introductions were made, and Ruby behaved impeccably with them all. The group moved away, continuing whatever conversation they'd been having before Harry and Ruby arrived, leaving Leo with them.

"Jolly good to see you, man." Leo cocked his head at Harry. "Seems an age since last weekend. Bloody bugger of a working week just gone. Damn court cases just wouldn't stop coming. Couple of times you'd have laughed, though. I wanted to smack the devils with the gavel for being in my courtroom at all. Still, that's me done until Wednesday now, and even then if we get another large snowfall I suspect some cases will be postponed." He cleared his throat. "So, you've come to show off your sub?"

"Uh, no." Harry turned to smile at Ruby, who gave him a wide one of her own. "She's not quite ready for that yet."

Leo clapped him on the back. "But you'll soon have her shipshape and raring to go, yes?"

Harry shrugged. "I'm not sure. What do you think, Ruby?" He placed his arm around her waist and held her tight, looking down at her. "Would you prefer to watch some play before you decide?"

She blushed a wonderful shade of pink. "I...I don't know. I think so, yes."

"Fabulous!" Leo said. "It's always a joy to see new subs become so comfortable with their Dom they can perform for us." He leant forwards, between Harry's and Ruby's heads. "Don't tell anyone, but it always makes me get a lump in my throat."

He drew back, winking, and Ruby let out a tinkle of laughter. Leo would get Harry's thanks later for putting her so at ease, but the shuffle of several feet behind him indicated tonight's meeting was about to begin.

"Is there definitely a show on tonight?" Harry asked.

"Isn't there always? You know this lot. If there isn't one scheduled, someone always steps up to the plate." Leo stared at the stage. "But I had an invitation delivered. You?" He turned back to face Harry and raised his eyebrows.

"I did. New equipment." Harry felt better someone else had received the unusual summons.

"Yes, and I wonder what the devil it is!" Leo smiled broadly. "I can see, if it's a good piece, a scrabble to be the first to use it tonight."

Harry laughed, stroking Ruby's lower back. He was concerned at how quiet she was, realising it must be somewhat daunting to be a new person among so many friends. He nodded to Leo and led her to the back row of chairs.

"We'll keep out of the way in case you don't like it," he said, pulling her down into the seat beside him. "We can leave without disturbing the others."

"Okay." She gripped his hand. "Leo was friendly."

"He always is. Seems he's let his sub go and is on the lookout for another."

Did it hurt him to release her like it will when I let Ruby go?

"So you're both teachers, then?" she asked.

"Yes, two of the only seven here, in fact. Everyone else is a proper couple."

"I'd love to be a proper couple," she said, gazing at him and squeezing his hand.

"I think I'm rather leaning towards that myself these days."

That was all he'd give her, the only indication he was feeling something more for her other than the relationship they'd initially agreed on. He couldn't influence her any more than that. It wouldn't be fair. She had to choose him herself, and for the right reasons. He would have to judge whether she'd made the correct decision if she wanted to be with him.

He stared at her lovely elfin face, at the hope in her eyes and the pretty smile on her lips.

Let her choose me. Jesus Christ let her choose me…

He looked away, at the stage, unable to gaze at her for fear of giving himself away. Everyone had taken their seats — around forty or so people — and the club owner, the beautiful and elegant blonde Laura Stiles, stood behind the podium.

"Welcome, everyone," she said, forty-year-old features appearing so much younger. "As you're aware, tonight is somewhat special due to a member — who wishes to remain anonymous — donating a very large and expensive piece of equipment. Because this is such an alluring item, I decided to have a draw before the meeting to determine who uses it first. The donator picked a winner out of the hat, so to speak, and I'm delighted to announce Harry Knowles and his guest are the lucky winners."

Harry widened his eyes in shock as Ruby gasped and all heads turned to look at them. He nodded, acknowledging the win. "We won't be using it unless you're happy to do so," he whispered to Ruby, putting his free hand on her knee as he looked at her. "All right?"

She nodded, biting her lip.

"Good."

"Now," Laura said, slapping her palm on the podium top. "Before the equipment is revealed, let us do our usual weekly question and answer, and then we have a wonderful couple coming up to the stage to show what they've discovered this past week. I assure you it should be delightful. So, any questions?"

Master stood behind the curtain on the stage, hidden from everyone's view. He seethed, tuning out the question-and-answer session, thinking about what he'd overheard before Laura came on stage. Ruby. What an utter load of rubbish. Either she'd conned Knowles into thinking that was what she was called or they'd made it up between them.

Margaret—*that* was her name, goddamn it—was radiant, and it grated on his last nerve. She'd never looked like that with him these past few years, always appearing drab, tired and ugly. He'd instructed her to make herself more presentable, and bar putting on a touch of make-up, she'd ignored him. A thorough beating with a cane hadn't ensured she wore the clothes he'd bought her, the spike-heeled boots or the PVC bra that gave a tantalising display of her nipples through the circular cut-out. Which was why he'd bought that equipment. To teach her that he called the shots—not her. He was the one who said what she wore and how she looked.

He stared at her, grinding his teeth until his gums hurt. She glowed, the pink blush on her cheeks becoming, her body movements fluid—none of the stiffness she'd exhibited around him. So Knowles was good for her, Master could admit that—grudgingly—but she didn't belong with him. She was Master's, body and soul, and he'd do everything in his power to ensure things went back to the way they were.

He missed punishing her.

He squinted, trying to make out her features, but she sat too far away. Her hand in Knowles' pissed him off, and he recalled how her skin felt, how soft it was. How it scarred so easily. His cock twitched, and he fought the urge to rub it through his trousers. He'd save his hard-on for later, when he had her where he wanted her.

Smiling, he crept towards the back of the stage, keeping to the shadows and praying no one caught his movement. Pleased that his plan was working perfectly, he took the exit and followed the corridor that led outside. There, he closed the door behind him and sucked in a huge lungful of icy air. Careful of his steps in the snow, he walked around the front of the building and entered the foyer as though he'd only just arrived. Veronica, the uptight bitch, tried hard to hide her sneer but failed. He signed in, headed for the hallway, and sidled into the meeting room.

His sights went straight to Ruby, who still clutched Knowles' hand and seemed caught up in whatever discussion was going on. No one turned to look at him. Relieved, he went upstairs to wait, more than ready for the next phase of his plan to begin.

Chapter Eleven

Ruby watched the scene playing out before her, but in truth her mind was occupied elsewhere. The woman on stage was being fucked by two very large Masters and they were making her beg for it. The scene did nothing for her — she didn't like the thought of having more than one man, liking the thought of only Harry so much better.

Swallowing past the ball of emotion clogging her throat, she glanced at Harry. She wanted to make him proud so he wouldn't want to get rid of her in a couple of weeks. How could she prove to him how much he meant to her already? Shit, she was in love with a guy she barely knew and didn't even want to contemplate life without him anymore.

He put his hand on her knee and her heart skipped a beat. Every touch she craved, further proof of his acceptance of her. The scene was fast coming to a close and she looked forward to seeing the end just so she could have some alone time with Harry.

The club and all the people seemed great, nothing like her previous Master had said about the Doms and subs he interacted with. Sighing, she watched Harry stroke the sensitive skin on her knee. Her pussy responded and although she wanted to please him, she returned her attention to the stage.

The two Doms ordered the little sub to come and seconds later the vocal appreciation of their explosion erupted throughout the room.

Harry got up and talked with a couple of people in the row in front. Then he took her hand and she rose, following behind him towards some other men, keeping her head down. She didn't want to draw any attention to herself, and when Harry started a new conversation with the men, she didn't listen. Her heart hammered—they were going to go and test out the new equipment—and she panicked at the thought of what it could be. So many times Master had brought home some new 'toy' that meant she would be in for hours of torture. Her pulse jumping beneath her skin, she tried to calm her nerves.

Harry won't keep you if you don't show him your worth. You can do this, Ruby—just breathe through it and try to enjoy.

A man handed Harry a key for the dungeon then kissed her knuckles before moving away to join others. Closing her eyes briefly, she opened them again and followed Harry's lead towards the door. A couple of other guests stopped him to have a word, and one or two admired his new sub. Ruby hated their gazes. She wasn't a piece of meat on display. She was for Harry and no one else.

She relaxed the moment they were out of the room.

"Tell me what's wrong?" he asked, stroking her cheek.

Ruby turned to him, opened her mouth then shut it. "Nothing." She didn't want to be a disappointment, and how many times had Master told her that she had been?

"Ruby honey, please, I don't want you to be uncomfortable around me. Please tell me what's wrong so I can help."

Closing her eyes again, she tried to form the right words. "I'm nervous."

Oh, fucking great. Out of all the words you can come up with to explain your issues, you come up with, I'm nervous.

You can do better.

"I understand." He cupped her cheek, tilting her head back. "Ruby, I'm not some sadist. I won't get pleasure out of your distress. I want you to feel safe with me. If at any point you're feeling nervous say your safe word. You remember your safe word?"

She nodded.

"Say it for me so I can hear it and know you'll say it if I take it too far."

"Isn't that against the rules?"

Harry shook his head. "No, not my rules. I like to know my sub can trust me enough to use their safe word. I'll stop and it doesn't mean the end of our exploration."

His posh words really turned her on. She could listen to him talk all night long.

"Butter."

"See, sounded good to hear it."

Ruby smiled and whispered the word again. Harry pressed her up against the wall, making her cry out seconds before his lips descended on hers. She moaned when his tongue plundered and she met him halfway. He kissed the hell out of her then reared back.

"You're a bad little sub," he whispered.

Ruby shivered as he cupped her arse beneath her skirt.

"You feel so damn good," he said.

She'd got to see a whole other side of him, like the club truly transformed him into a Dominant, and she shivered in anticipation of his coming punishment, to be under his hand as he dished out his pleasure.

"Thank you, Sir."

She gripped a fistful of his hair, bringing his lips back to hers. Their kisses grew fiery and passionate. Ruby was so close to begging him to take her there and then but at the last minute, Harry pulled away.

Without saying a word, he took her up a flight of stairs to the dungeon. Doors dotted the passage, and he produced the key he'd been given. She watched him slide it into the lock and activate the code, which opened the door.

"This is a pretty secure place," she said.

"I'm sure you noticed some of the more important people of our society walking around downstairs. It costs to be this privileged and gives members the privacy they want."

He shut the door and Ruby took the time to look around the massive dungeon. A four-poster bed stood in the corner with a chest of drawers beside it, and through a doorway was an en suite.

"The club supplies everything for the couple or party on the night. Domination isn't just about the sex act but about the complete caring of a Dominant for his sub. The bathroom has all the essentials to bathe and care after punishments and sex."

Ruby rubbed her arms, suddenly feeling cold. "It's a little...out of my league."

Being in places like this forcefully reminded her of how different she was from him. The first flat she'd rented hadn't had this type of luxury, and yet this served as a room for people who paid a yearly membership.

Harry circled her waist and pressed his arm against her back.   "You're not out of your league."

"Harry, look at me. Shit, listen to me, for God's sake. I'm common and used to earn minimum wage. I don't have a degree or any type of university education." She could list so much more but oncoming tears had her biting her lip.

"You think I care about that?"

Ruby shrugged. She didn't know anymore.

For the first time the silence between them was awkward. She wished with all of heart she was different.

"Ruby, I don't care about the differences between us. I don't want you to be anyone other than who you are, and when you decide you want to leave...it...it will hurt me."

Ruby spun in his arms. He looked really upset at the prospect of her going.

"I don't want to go," she said.

He nodded. "Why don't we leave all of the normal conversations for later when we're in the privacy of home?"

Harry took her hand and led her through the small room to where the new piece of equipment was covered by a large black sheet.

"Ready?"

They each took a corner of the sheet and unveiled the device.

"What is it?" she asked.

Harry let her go and went and looked at the caged equipment. Rubbing her arms again, she glanced back at the door, wondering if she ought to leave, just go so she didn't make a fool of herself when she wasn't able to be what he wanted in here.

"Come here, honey."

Ruby went to him. The cage had leather straps for the feet and hands so a person would be spread out fully, star-shaped. Harry opened the prison-like door, and from its width she could tell that if whoever was inside wanted to get out fast they would struggle.

"It's a perfect fit for you. Do you want to go in?" Harry asked.

Did she? Although a little awed by the piece, she did want to go in...for him. She nodded and walked through the doorway sideways, as did Harry, who almost got stuck he was so large. He urged her towards the straps, and she stood in position, heart beating so fast she worried she might be sick. Excitement played a big part, as well as fear of the unknown. Harry might well show a harder side to himself here, but her instinct was to trust him.

He bound her wrists and ankles. "It was like it was built for you," he muttered, seemingly to himself.

He shut the door and Ruby froze. This was the perfect piece of equipment to guarantee the person inside would be stuck until their Master let them out.

"I've never seen anything like it before," he said, hand to his chin.

He frowned and Ruby couldn't determine if that was a good or bad thing.

"Could...you...please...open...?" She stopped to lick her lips, her heart racing faster. She could cope having the straps on, but the door shutting, the enclosed space sent her over the edge and into a world of panic. "Please...open."

Harry opened the door immediately and untied her. Ruby rushed out, grabbing her chest as she fought to bring her breathing under control. He held her through her panic attack.

"I've got you," he whispered, stroking her hair and face.

She calmed down after a short time and was able to turn and face him. "Please, never shut the door on that thing again."

"Okay. I never will."

"Do you want to try again?" she asked.

Harry glanced between the equipment and her. She saw he wanted to but took her hand and brought her flush with him.

"Soon. Dance with me?"

She softened against him, resting her head on his chest. "We've got no music."

"We don't need any."

What was it about him that made her melt?

They danced together in one spot and Ruby closed her eyes, loving the feeling of closeness the moment brought. He surrounded her in his warmth and she never wanted to let him go. Would she ever be the right woman for him? The type of woman he could settle down with?

Her heart ached to think of him with someone else, and if she had to change completely to be with him, then she'd do it. Her feelings for him deepened with every passing minute.

She opened her eyes and looked at the terrifying device, so like something Master would have made for her. He derived great pleasure in keeping her cooped up in one place. The old images of her past pressed in on her, of being tied up and bound for hours, her pleads for release going unheard or ignored.

He'd relished the fear on her face when he'd brought out the rope and taken her to the basement that time. When he wasn't at work, he'd keep her tied to the bed for as long as possible—sometimes the entire three days from Friday evening to Monday morning.

She saw all these harsh punishments that could be administered with her strapped to the device, but with Harry's arms around her she didn't need to worry. He would keep her safe and she trusted him with more than her body. Harry was the type of man she could trust with her heart and mind.

Taking a breath, she pulled away and stared at him. He truly was an amazing man, and he cared for her. She could see it and feel it with every move and touch. There was nothing cruel about his domination, and seeing this, knowing this, made her want to be the perfect submissive for him.

It was another barrier to break down, to overcome, and then she would see the power of being with a man who truly cared about her.

"I'm ready to go back in," she said.

Harry didn't move but watched her. "Are you sure about this?"

"I trust you, Harry. This is about us, not the device and not...and not him. I want to do this and prove to myself the fucking bastard could rot in hell for all I care. I want to be with you every step of the way." She took another breath, knowing she was rambling on.

"I don't want you to think you have to do anything you don't want to, Ruby."

"I understand, and besides, I've always got butter if I want you to stop at any time."

They both smiled and Harry pulled her against him again, kissing her lips.

"You're amazing, you know that?" he said.

She nodded. "Because of you I'm starting to think it. Maybe one day I might believe it too."

Harry got her to strip naked and then helped her back into the cage, removing his pristine white shirt in the process. He looked like some Greek god in his black trousers, his defined chest muscles highlighted with every turn under the soft light. Ruby was already wet just from looking at the perfection of his partially naked form. No man should look that good.

He took her hands first, staring into her eyes as he cuffed first one wrist then the other, testing the give of the straps. He kissed her again after the second strap fit snugly.

"You look so beautiful, naked and bound."

With the way he was staring, she *felt* fucking beautiful. She bowed her head in subservience and watched him go to his knees and take first one foot then the other until she was strapped in place, awaiting whatever pleasure or punishment he chose to give.

"From now on, in here you'll call me Sir or Master. Any other name will result in a punishment, do I make myself clear?"

Her pussy quivered with excitement, his demands making her hot and horny.

"Yes...Sir."

Ruby wanted to see him lose control, to see what happened when the true Master in him took over. But she waited—this was still new territory to her.

Master would have punished her severely by now.

Harry went to the closet outside the cage and pulled out a whip, some gel and a few other little toys and trinkets. He returned to her and dribbled the lotion on his hands. Starting from the bottom up, he rubbed her skin, massaging. She moaned as each muscle was stimulated by his careful attention, her cream dampening the inside of her thighs as he moved further up her leg.

"You're already dripping wet for me, little sub. Do you like what I'm doing?"

I fucking love it.

"Yes, Sir," she panted out, her head suddenly heavy and her limbs needing the tightness of the straps to keep her upright.

Once he was done with her legs, he moved up her body, bypassing her cunt, which so needed his careful devotion. She moaned in frustration. She wanted his fingers in her slit and would do anything for him to stop the burning ache deep inside.

Instead, he continued on, chuckling, hands on her belly then skating up her ribs and petting her breasts. Her nipples were erect and pulsing, his touch making her wince from the intense pleasure.

"You're so responsive."

Ruby couldn't even drum up a comeback. Her body was on fire with demanding need, all from a simple massage. It was embarrassing and stimulating at the same time.

Harry knew how to work her body to make her crave his touch—and oh, the delightfully wicked possibilities he could create...

Without the fear of the unknown, she was able to immerse herself in the moment and trust what was about to happen. Harry didn't treat her as a piece of meat but as a person.

"Now, sub, I think I should have a little taste of you."

He nipped her mouth playfully and Ruby opened up for him. He plunged his tongue inside and finally touched her creamy cunt. She groaned, trying to thrust her hips towards him but with him pressed against her, she met with the back of the cage. The ability to use all parts of the body in here was hindered by the cage's rear. She supposed if Harry wanted to punish her on the arse he could unstrap her and turn her around.

"Ruby, you're dripping onto my fingers." He teased her open and inserted a finger into her warmth.

She so wanted to give him as much pleasure as he was giving her but her bound hands prevented it.

"I could play with you all night, sub."

Ruby whimpered when he fingered her clit. She really could give this man anything he desired. She loved him so fucking much already. Love—absolutely, completely and without a shadow of a doubt. Other people needed time to analyse their feelings or to come to terms with a change of relationship, but Ruby trusted her head and body, and most importantly, she trusted her heart.

Harry was the one for her.

The newfound knowledge allowed her to open up and give herself over to the lust and fire Harry caused.

A buzzer sounded on the door, interrupting their play.

"What's that?" she asked.

Harry cursed quietly. "I don't know, but they'd better have a good excuse."

She loved being his, being wanted by him. He kissed her again before going to the little intercom on the wall beside the main door.

"What?" he snapped. "I hope you know it's against the rules to interrupt a high-ranking member's dungeon time unless it's absolutely necessary."

He sounded so smart and clever.

"I'm so sorry, sir," came a nervous female voice, "but there's been an urgent call placed through to your number. The one that states we must disturb you."

Ruby sighed.

"Give me a minute." He shut the intercom off and came over to her. "I've got to go and answer this call. I won't be a moment, but the door will be locked and no one can get in besides me. I'll take you down so you can get a drink from the cabinet over there while I'm gone." He moved to untie the cuffs.

"You won't be long, and like you said, no one can get in. I trust you, Harry. I'll be fine here. Leave me tied."

"Are you sure?"

"You're wasting time." She laughed.

Harry kissed her lips and then left her. She watched him go and heard the lock connecting.

I'm really doing this. I'm in love with Harry Knowles.

She giggled, so happy and contented. Finally she could give someone her love and not be terrified of having them smash her heart.

When they went back to his house, she'd tell him her real name. Margaret Savage. She cringed. Maybe she could get it changed legally.

The lock clicked back on the main door and she smiled, looking up, excited to continue their scene.

Ruby froze, her body tightening. Fear consumed her.

It wasn't Harry at all.

"Hello, Margaret."

Chapter Twelve

Master stared at Margaret, narrowing his eyes at the way she'd been bound. Knowles hadn't taken advantage of the built-in chastity-like belt attached to the rear bars — one that had a hole for easy cock or toy insertion. It hung there beside her, useless.

What an utter waste of a good thing.

He gave her face his full attention while letting the door snap closed behind him, enjoying the sound it made. He fancied it was one of finality, a no-going-back-now click that signified his plan nearly coming to fruition. How he'd longed for this night, finding her here and letting her know she couldn't just walk away from him any time she chose. The days since she'd been gone had been long and annoying. Boring without her to torment. Well, she'd be gone no more.

He had limited time in which to slap her about a bit before releasing her, then getting her out of here and back to his house where she belonged.

Where she'd stay until he tired of her.

But maybe he wouldn't get tired. Maybe keeping her where he had in mind would amuse him for the rest of his life. Fuck, he could take on another sub and neither woman would know of the other's existence. He could strap the new one to the equipment he'd set up in the spare room once it arrived. He'd ordered a duplicate device for his home, and *this* time he'd paid extra to ensure the shop owner himself delivered it, snow or not. He'd also made it clear he wasn't going to be fucked about on this occasion. The other sub, Ruby, would be...there—out of sight, out of earshot, but close enough he could go to her when the fancy took him.

She glared back at him—yes, glared, the cheeky bitch—her initial fright gone now. If he was a good judge he'd say she was angry, indignant that he'd walked in and found her here.

Knowles had done quite a bit of damage, undoing Master's hard work.

Bastard.

Master lifted one hand to his chin and pinched it lightly, more to give her the idea he was amused by her anger than anything else. And it was no matter, really, her change in attitude. He'd enjoy re-teaching her all over again.

A knife and a threat or two worked wonders on some people.

"Harry will be back in a minute, you know," Margaret said.

Her facial expression was so smug he had to rein in the desire to go inside that cage and slap her cheek. But no, he couldn't do that. A handprint wouldn't look particularly fetching when they casually strode through the lobby on their way out—and it *would* be a casual stride. He'd make sure she understood the consequences if she didn't leave quietly and with a smile.

"I'm aware of that, Margaret, but I've made sure I have enough time to get us reacquainted before we leave."

"Fucked if I'm leaving with you," she snapped, clenching her fists.

"Well, now. Who went and ruined your manners? Let me guess..."

"No one ruined them—they were always like this until I met you."

She tipped her chin and continued to stare. She was a feisty one, he'd give her that. But feisty wasn't how he wanted her to be, how she *shouldn't* be, and over the coming week—because it would only take him a week to punish the belligerence out of her—she'd be back to normal.

Oh yes.

He sighed and walked into the cage. "It really doesn't become you, to be so brazen. It makes you look common."

"I *am* fucking common!" she shouted, cheeks reddening, eyes blazing. "And I'm proud of who I am. I shouldn't have to change to be what other people want. You should have accepted me as I was. Changing me the way you did... Shit, you're just a control freak, I see that now. You chose me, didn't you? Chose me because you knew I'd be easily manipulated." She laughed, a guttural, low chortle. "But not anymore. God, no. You'll never get to me like that again."

He eyed her for a few moments, hiding his insistent need to take one step forward and wrap his hands around her throat and squeeze until her eyes bulged. She really was tiresome with her self-importance, and if he allowed her to annoy him much more he'd hurt her here—now.

That wasn't an option.

I must stick to the plan. She's uncouth again, has the idea she's got choices, but that's quite all right. Nothing I can't solve.

He raised one hand and stroked her cheek, gratified to see she was unable to hide a flinch. Beneath that bravado she was still afraid of him, then.

Good.

"You know," he said, thumbing her lips, "you look delightful trussed up like this. The only thing that would make this scene perfect is if you had the belt on. I'm surprised Knowles didn't strap you up with it. Surprised he didn't fuck you while you couldn't move anything except your hands, feet and head. And look"—he rattled a band of leather attached to a rear bar by a chain—"this would have stopped the head movements." His cock hardened. "Totally at one's mercy..."

Her jaw muscles pulsed and her breathing grew heavier. He leant forwards to sniff her, smelling strange bathing aromas and...Knowles.

That just wouldn't do.

He took two steps back and punched her in the stomach, loving the way she automatically tried to bring herself into a ball and failing. Loving the strangled grunt that left her pretty little mouth. Loving, loving, loving the way she had a touch of the old Margaret in her eyes as she looked at him— eyebrows raised, eyes wide and brimming with the usual boring question—*why*?

Satisfaction streamed through him, and his cock ached. "Now that you understand we're completely back to normal, I'm going to release you, Margaret.

Before I do, though, there are certain rules. You *must* obey them. If you don't, there won't only be consequences for *you* regarding punishment."

"Fuck you!" She spat in his face. "Fuck you and the scabby horse you rode in on, arsehole!"

Oh dear. This is an...unfortunate turn of events.

He wiped her spittle from his cheek with his sleeve. Sighed. Fisted his hands and resisted thumping her in the stomach again. He so wanted to hear that pained grunt...

"Let me explain this a little better, Margaret, hmmm? I'm going to release you, and you're going to get dressed very quickly. We're going to leave this room—you'll be handcuffed to me—and you're going to smile and walk beside me as though you're happy. We're going to exit this building and get into my car—"

"I'm not going with you. Harry will be here in a minute and—"

"Harry will *not* be here in a minute!" he roared into her face. "Harry is...detained. If you don't leave with me in the way I've described, he'll be detained permanently. Do I make myself clear?"

She gasped and finally, *finally* tugged at the binds.

Achilles heel. Marvellous!

"What have you done to him? Where is he?"

"You needn't concern yourself with trifling details."

He released one wrist and one ankle, then grabbed her free arm while he took care of the other ankle restraint. Pressing against her to keep her from struggling or lashing out, he undid the last manacle. He stepped back and dragged her to her clothing, standing over her as she dressed, amused that she kept glancing at the door.

"Believe me, he's not coming, Margaret. Now hurry up before I lose my temper."

He kicked her calf and she stumbled but made no sound.

A pity...

She made short work of dressing then, and once finished stood in front of him with her arm out for him to snap on the cuffs. At last, she was seeing sense.

"I'm not doing this because I'm obeying you like I did before," she said. "I'm doing it for Harry."

"Oh, how delightfully sweet. Margaret is in love." He yanked her towards the door. "Just so we're clear before I open this door... If you call out, look at anyone with an expression that makes it clear you're not happy, or you mess me around while in this building, Harry will stop breathing. Understand?"

She nodded, her face paling.

Master sighed. She really had lost her manners.

He took a good amount of flesh on her upper arm between his finger and thumb and pinched. "I said, understand?"

"Yes, Sir." She winced.

"It hurt to say that, didn't it?"

She didn't respond, just stared back at him with defiance written all over her.

Bitch.

He opened the door and escorted her down into the lobby, watching her in his peripheral. She smiled over-brightly, and one or two people sitting on the sofas glanced their way, some with heads cocked in silent question as to what Margaret was doing with him, others with grins, completely unaware she had arrived with Knowles. The former didn't bother him if they thought to alert Knowles of their leaving. Master would have Margaret right where he wanted her at his place long before Knowles got a whiff of his sub being taken.

His sub? Mine. Mine!

They breezed past the receptionist and went outside, Margaret sucking in a breath—the shock of the cold, he supposed. Once out of sight of the club entrance, Master took her around the corner into the car park, roughly shepherding her to his vehicle. He pressed her inside with his hand on her head, treating her like the criminal she was. She'd broken the law, his law, and she'd now have to pay the price and do the time.

Chuckling at his thoughts, he unlocked the cuff on his wrist and secured her to the handle on the inside of the door. He'd anticipated her clawing at his face with her free hand as he strapped her in, but she remained still, gaze fixed out the windshield.

He locked her inside and walked around to get in himself. The engine purred to life, and Master imagined Margaret's reaction when she realised where she would be doing her penance. She hated the room underground, the one he'd built himself below his back garden, even though she'd only been in there once and for an hour or so.

This time she'd be in there a damn sight longer.

He drove, mind on the next phase of his plan, a part of him vigilant to any tricks she might decide to pull while on their journey. He needn't have worried. She sat like a good girl the whole way home, dry-eyed and silent. He noted goosebumps on her arms—he hadn't bothered putting on the heater—and saw her quivering chin as she trembled. From the cold or fear?

Either way he didn't care. Her feelings no longer came into it, and when he thought about it, they hadn't before either. Why should they? She was his to do with as he wished and no one would convince him otherwise. He laughed at that—a wonderful belly laugh that cleansed him, eased out the kinks in his muscles and smoothed the jagged edges of his nerves.

He pulled to a stop in his driveway and got out, uncuffing her from the handle and pushing her to his front door. Inside, he continued guiding her from behind until they stood in the dining room. He'd moved the table and chairs over to the side earlier, easily shifting them due to the rug beneath, and now the trap door to the underground room was in plain view, open and ready to accept her.

"You know where you're going, don't you, Margaret?"

She nodded, not a frisson of fear evident, gaze unwavering, chin set, mouth an angry slash that made him want to hurt her. Time enough for that later. For now, keeping her below the ground would appease his anger. He rather looked forward to imagining her crying down there, pining for a man she'd never have again. Oh, the heartbreak! Oh, the sublime pleasure of seeing her twisted up in pain—inside and out!

He bobbed his head in the direction of the trap door and she moved closer to it without complaint, taking the wooden steps down into the darkness. He followed, battling with the voice inside his head telling him to push her, let her tumble over the steps and land on the cement floor.

At the bottom, he reached out to his right and found the hanging light cord. He tugged it and a low-watt bulb sprang to life, illuminating the tunnel-like passageway where a metal door stood at the end. Margaret walked towards it, back straight, spine full of the courage he'd beat out of her, perhaps tomorrow, perhaps next week. He hadn't decided yet.

Once they reached the door, she moved to one side so he could insert the key. He shoved her into the large room, bare of any comforts, the floor the same rough concrete as the tunnel, the walls coarse, unpainted beige plaster.

The perfect prison.

She walked to the centre and turned to face him, eyes blank and giving nothing away, her body seemingly at ease. He wondered if she was screaming inside, imagining where Harry was and why her gallant knight hadn't yet come to find her. Whether he would even bother once he discovered she wasn't in the dungeon cage anymore. Master anticipated a visit from him, one where he allowed Knowles into his home to search for Margaret, laughing with glee inside when he showed him into the dining room, the man completely unaware the entrance to finding her was right beneath the rug.

Master laughed—hard and hearty.

"Goodbye, Margaret. I'll be back at some point to check whether you're sorry. If I find you're not, I'll leave you again. Eventually, you'll give in and comply. Hunger and thirst will see to that. And oh"— he rubbed his arms in an exaggerated manner—"it's awfully chilly down here, don't you think?" He glanced around. "And no blankets or anything. Oh dear."

He backed out, studying her one last time before he closed the door.

When he returned later, he would expect that look of hatred to be gone, replaced with relief that he'd come back to let her out.

Chapter Thirteen

Ruby watched as Master closed the door on her prison. Although this was only the second time she'd been down here, memories from the last time came flooding back. How long did he intend keeping her here? It could be an indefinite length of time — no one, as far as she knew, was aware of this basement — and she realised no one except Harry would miss her. She'd cut herself off from her mother because of Master, so Ruby being incarcerated for months on end wouldn't be noticed.

A horrible thought hit her then. What if Master's friends knew of this room? What if he told them she was here and had the insane idea of sharing her with them? He'd shown possessive tendencies in the past, so she could only hope he still wanted to keep her for himself, but she didn't know him, not really, and with Master, anything was possible.

Having him touch her again had almost made her sick. In his car, she'd gone inside herself, to that place she'd inhabited before she met Harry, where she kept her *self* secure, away from Master. When he'd beaten her, put his hands all over her, his fingers in places she didn't want them to be, she'd switched off. Now, though, down here, she struggled to reach that safe place. Having been caressed in a wholly different way by Harry, she couldn't seem to erase Master's recent handling. Shuddering against a wave of revulsion, she simply stared at the wall, her body dead inside and in hateful contrast, alive on the outside with his touch. It was still on her, a tangible imprint of his hands on her skin, buzzing and squirming as though alive.

Unable to stand thinking about it anymore, she turned her mind to other things—anything to keep herself occupied.

What has he done to Harry? Is he okay?

She couldn't bear to think about anything happening to the man she loved. Had she fucked up big-time in keeping hers and Master's identities a secret?

Maybe I should have told Harry who I am, who Master is. He would know, then, where to come and find me, but now? Shit!

Panic settled in her gut, a heavy stone that exploded into fragments and spread to the rest of her body. She shook from the force of it and folded her arms, hands over her elbows in an attempt to stop the shivers. Her teeth chattered, the sound reverberating inside her head, and she closed her eyes to ward off the beginnings of a stress headache that threatened, a nasty little twitch at the base of her skull that would bloom and spread much like the panic had done until she gave in and huddled in the corner. She didn't know what to do or what to think and turned on the spot, knowing there was no way out except through that door. Master—

Stop calling him fucking Master. He's a pompous prick who deserves a kick in the teeth for what he's done. Call him by his proper, shitty fucking name!

She blew out a breath, pleased she hadn't caved in, that she still had fight left in her. She had Harry to focus on, to live for, and if Master thought he could break her again, he had another think coming.

To make herself angry, she thought of the real name of the man who had almost succeeded in turning her into a shell of her former self. Nigel. The prick used to disappear for hours on end, and now she knew it was most probably to the club. But shouldn't members of the club be under some kind of code? How had he been able to get away with taking her like that? Hadn't it been clear she was Harry's sub? Why hadn't someone stepped forward and stopped her leaving with Nigel? Or was that how it worked there, men and women could arrive with one person and leave with another? From her understanding, though, when a sub belonged to a Master, they remained with that Master until they were released, until their collar —

Fuck. She no longer wore a collar...

There was no way Nigel could have done anything to Harry, was there? Not at the club. He must have been bluffing. She'd noticed there were cameras all over the place, and someone must have seen what happened — or at least they would when the videos were looked over.

But do they even watch the videos? How long will it take for them to see what happened? It could be a weekly thing where they scan the footage. I could be here for days!

Fuck. She was such a fucking dim-witted idiot. Yes, she'd agreed to leave with him because of his threats to Harry, but would Nigel really have seen them through if she'd let someone know she was leaving against her will? She'd been convinced back then he would have, but now she wasn't so sure. He was just a bully towards women, only able to threaten and hurt them. If it came to standing up to a man, she wasn't convinced he had the balls.

Smacking her head with her hand, she cursed everything she could think of. The weather, the day, even the bloody time. There was no way he would have hurt Harry.

Going to the door, she tightened her hand around the metal knob, jerked and twisted it, anything to make a noise. But what was the point? Only Nigel would hear it, and knowing she was trying to get out would undoubtedly give him some kind of sadistic pleasure.

Despite that, she kicked the door and screamed at the empty, dark room.

"You fucking coward!" she yelled at the top of her voice.

Not caring about the pain, she continued to kick the door, to rant and curse the bloody thing for not opening. She'd get out of here somehow, get away from Nigel again if it was the last thing she did. For once in her life she was going to stand up to this bastard.

"Come back here, you prick!"

She slapped her palms on the door, wincing at the sting.

"See! I'm talking like a tramp. Come down here and beat it out of me. Make me speak like a lady if that's what gets you off. Come on, Nigel!"

Calling him by his name gave her a sense of control, of liberation. It would piss him off, possibly get him flinging that trapdoor open and barrelling down here, rage fuelling his steps.

"You're nothing like Harry, do you hear me? Nothing! He's a real Master. Knows how to paddle my arse properly. Not like you!"

Anger and rage built inside her, and she continued throwing taunts and insults until she heard the unmistakable sound of a key turning in the lock.

She was ready for this. Nothing like a rude awakening for a person to suddenly open up and take notice of the abuse they'd suffered. And fuck had she suffered.

No more!

The door swung open, and she stared at him, wondering if she rushed at him whether she'd catch him off guard for long enough to make it along that tunnel and up the steps. He filled the doorway, put his hands on the jamb either side of him, anticipating what she'd planned to do.

Shit.

"So," he said. "You refuse to behave."

He closed the door, locked it, then walked towards her. Ruby refused to look away or give in to the fear that had returned, bluntly and without warning. Facing him took a great amount of risk and courage, but she'd do it. She'd get out of here, find Harry, and tell him exactly what had happened. He was a lawyer—he'd help her bring charges against this sick fucker, wouldn't he? She swallowed past the knot in her throat and glared at him harder, pure defiance against the man and his regime.

"What have I told you, Margaret?"

"How a Master is not supposed to act."

He bit his lip, in an attempt to contain his anger she'd bet. Enlightenment hit her and she finally, *truly* saw past his suave outfit, his impeccable outer appearance, to the brute beneath the surface.

"I see Knowles has been filling your head with rubbish. The whole 'A sub is the true Master in any relationship' bullshit."

Ruby refused to bite back. It would serve this man right to be at the other end of a beating, to have the whip lash out at him and beat the living shit out of his hide, but now wasn't the time. She'd wait, see how things went and choose the right moment to strike.

"I'm going to have to train you from the start again." He shook his head as though weary.

She no longer cared what he thought. No one was going to destroy her ability to speak her mind or be a true sub with all the power.

"He is the better man," she said.

Nigel lashed out, slapping her cheek with such force her head snapped to the side. The contact stung — Jesus, it stung — but she refused to cry out. He turned abruptly and left the room, locking the door behind him.

Had she succeeded in getting one over on him? Had she actually rattled him?

She had no time to think further. The key scraped in the lock again and he slid back inside, a baseball bat in hand. He relocked the door, put the key in his pocket, and she wondered whether she could get it out at some point. She backed away to the rear wall, ready to defend herself from the blows that were sure to come. He advanced towards her, too fast for her to knock him down, grab the key and rush for the door.

"He is not the better man!" he screamed, smashing the bat against the wall beside her head.

She opened her mouth to scream insults back at him, but he gripped her throat with his free hand and squeezed. Her heart rate soared, and she breathed through her nose, short, shallow intakes of air that weren't enough for her greedy lungs. She went to wrestle his hand away but the thought of touching him stopped her. She sensed he wouldn't kill her, that he was just doing this to show her who was boss. And what was a squeeze around her throat? Nothing compared to the shit he'd put her through before.

"You fucking bitch." He brought his face inches from hers. "You're my woman, my slut, and I'll use you however I desire." He smacked the bat on the wall again and a split from the impact made a deep crevice down the bat's length.

It showed Ruby the true extent of Nigel's aggression, how he expected to possess her in every way.

He's fucking crazy!

"You know, you're so desperate for him to love you..." Nigel laughed, the sound out of place and scary. "If he figures out I'm your Master, if he comes here to rescue your sorry little arse, all it will take is a few words from me for him to believe you've gone back to your whore of a mother. Yes, I'll tell him you've gone back to your mother's. He'll buy it. He'll see your childhood home, see where you came from, what and who you really are, a scumbag common bitch!" He breathed over her face and waited for her to respond.

She held back a shudder from the warm, stinking air hitting her skin. "It doesn't matter," she croaked out. "Harry said he loves me exactly as I am."

But it does matter what Harry thinks of me. It does. I love him with all my heart and would do anything for him, but if he goes to my mother's and sees...I'll lose him. No matter what he's said about my past, how it makes no difference to him, I'll lose him...

She couldn't give in to her fear, though, and right now she had to think about her safety. All she wanted was get out of here without any trouble—but if she had to fight she would.

"Let me go," she choked out. "You can find another person who wants to be your special someone."

Reason with him. Play up to his narcissistic side.

"There's someone out there who will worship the ground you walk on, Nigel. Why do you want me?" God, her throat throbbed from his hold. Her voice was coming out odd, broken and raspy. "I'll never be able to give you what you want, so what's the point? Don't you want adoration? A woman who thinks you're a god?"

That's exactly what he wants, but he's hell-bent on making me be that person. Jesus, what was I thinking when I first met up with him? Why didn't I see him for who he really is?

"Do you think I want to train someone new, woman? Why should I bother when it will only take a week or so to have you back to normal? I don't deny I could have any woman I wanted, but you—you're something special. There's something about you... I enjoy you hating me, Margaret. When you showed signs of caring for me at the start, didn't you notice how I beat it out of you? And this is where you're dumb. Another woman might have realised what I was doing, but not you. No, you hated me even more, doing just what I'd planned all along. Your hate makes my cock hard." He pulled the key out of his pocket and dropped the bat, kicking it out of reach. "I'm going to show you how special it can be between us, how that hate of yours can make my cock so hard you'll think I'm fucking you with metal. And even *that* can be arranged..."

Ruby looked at the crazed man. How had he managed to get away with this shit for so long?

Because I let him. I played right into his hands. Fuck!

Licking her lips, she thought about her life with him over the past few years and couldn't find a single memory where the pain and torture had been a form of affection. Nigel was a sadist—nothing more and nothing less.

"We are going to play," he said, removing his hand from her throat and gripping her hair in his fist.

Ruby struggled to get out of his hold despite her earlier thoughts of remaining calm until she found a chink in his plan that would enable her to escape. Instinct took over and she made to run, not caring if she left a handful of her hair in his hand. He caught her around the waist and threw her against the wall. The pain in her temple from the contact was instant and shocked her system, but she wouldn't be contained. Even while her head ached and submitting seemed like the easiest option, at the same time she was determined to be free.

He thrust her up, hand to her throat again, blessed relief on her scalp as he let go of her hair. She gasped and lashed out, smacking the side of his head.

Nigel growled, covering the spot she'd hit. "That's it, you bitch. Hate me, hate me some more. My cock's hard for you, see that?"

Strength infused with revulsion filled her. She shoved at his chest and smacked at his arm until his hold on her throat weakened. She fought until he dropped his hand, then charged past him to the door, her legs wobbly, head pounding.

"Give me the fucking key!" she shouted, knowing her request would be denied. Why had she gone against her earlier plan? Why had she allowed instinct to overrule her like that? Yes, she needed to escape, to get out of this place, but he wasn't going to just hand over the key and allow her to walk away. She damned herself, could have kicked her own arse to kingdom come for this massive error. Now she'd just given him something else to get hard over, more hatred, more of what he wanted.

He stalked to her, grabbed her around the waist again and threw her against the wall next to the door, landing a punch to the side of her head. A cry erupted from her lips before she had a chance to stop it. Stars glittered, her vision faded, and she panicked at having lost control. She should have remembered what he was capable of, but her newfound confidence from being with Harry had masked the utter horror of her past with Nigel. God, she knew exactly what he could do, but now she was in the thick of it again, she realised some of his punishments had faded in her mind — the terrible nastiness of them, how they had hurt...

He clamped a hand around her throat again, menace clear on his face, the veins in his neck protruding through his skin.

She clawed his hands.

"Do you see what I can do to you? I can squeeze the life out of your useless hide. You mean nothing to me. Do you hear me? Nothing! You're just a vessel, a body I can abuse."

He stopped and Ruby couldn't think against the panic welling inside her.

I can't breathe.

"Now, we're going to go and play for a while. Let me make one thing clear, Margaret. You start any of your pathetic games, and I'll end you and the useless piece of shit you've been shacked up with. His friends will mourn his loss at first, but after a while no one will care. I will kill him, understand?"

Ruby knew now he was capable of anything. He was truly demented. She sagged and tried to think of any way out of her situation but couldn't handle the prospect of being killed or causing Harry any ill will…or death.

She nodded at him, the last swirls of breath left inside her almost gone.

His hold tightened a fraction before he let go.

"Good girl," he whispered.

Ruby collapsed to the floor, gasping for air, and once again vowed to get the hell away from him somehow. All she needed was time. And that baseball bat.

"Now, I think you need a little reflection time before we start playing, don't you?"

He knelt, caressed her cheek, and she had to hold back the flinch inside her. She thought of all the times she'd been in this same position, frightened and afraid.

This time was different. She wasn't only fighting for herself but fighting for Harry.

"I can't wait to fuck your cunt again and retrain you to be mine," he growled, slamming his lips down on hers.

He bit into her lips, demanding a response when she refused to kiss him back. She couldn't give him anything.

His teeth sunk further. She winced at the taste of blood. Nigel came up for air and looked at the damage he'd done. Arousal was clear in his eyes. She tried to cover her disgust but he must have seen it. He slapped her round the face repeatedly, her head going from side to side. Three to four slaps later, her face hot and her mind a mass of activity and revenge, he pushed her away.

"Now, I think an hour or so down here alone again should do it." He stood looking down at her. "Think about Harry, about how much you want him to live, because if you don't play this game properly, I *will* kill him."

He scooped up the baseball bat, unlocked the door and slammed it behind him. The sound of the key turning, the bolt hitting home, didn't make her feel despair as it may have in the past. No, it gave her strength. She'd get one over on him, have his arse hauled to court, have him brought to the stand to try and justify his treatment of her.

This time she wasn't going to break.

This time he'd see her hatred in glorious colours, bright and in his face.

Let's see if his cock gets hard over that!

Chapter Fourteen

Harry's head hurt. So much so he dared not open his eyes. Had he drunk too much brandy the night before? He couldn't remember, didn't even know what day it was. The thought that it was Monday and he was meant to be in the office snapped his eyes open, and for a second or two he was confused as to why he was in a small dungeon in the club until remembrance came crashing in on him.

"What the...?"

He jumped up, disoriented, the side of his head throbbing. His world tilted and he staggered to a stop at the door, one hand on the wall, the other to his temple. Nauseated, he recalled leaving Ruby in the cage to receive a phone call, then, upon finding no one on the other end, making his way to the meeting room so he could take the stairs and return to her. In the upper hallway someone had coughed behind him and he'd turned to see who it was. A rough sack had been jammed over his head before he had the chance to set eyes on anyone, his arms were yanked behind his back, and a large hand held his wrists together as he was propelled along. He'd heard a door open and close, and then a low male growl. He was thrust in the chest and seconds later a sharp, blinding pain shot through his head, sending him spiralling into darkness.

Which brought him to now.

He opened the door, lurching into the hallway, the dungeon Ruby was in opposite him. He patted his pocket in search of the key, panic setting in when he couldn't find it. Fear uncoiled in his gut, spreading far and wide—the kind of fear that left him weak, as though he was boneless, without substance. Someone had taken the key, no doubt about it, and he instinctually knew that someone had tricked him in order to get into Ruby's dungeon.

"Fuck!"

Although he knew it was futile, he tried the door, and was surprised when it flew open. The cage was empty—as empty as his mind for a second or two, where he didn't know what to do. Then that fear turned into anger and concern for Ruby's safety and there was no stopping him. He blundered back into the hallway, noting the security camera lenses had been blacked out. Incensed, he ran downstairs and into the meeting room, glancing around, pissed off as hell to see the space empty. He darted out and into the lobby, staring at a couple who necked on one of the sofas then switching his gaze to the desk. Veronica sat in her usual spot, staring at him as though he was a wild, crazed thing, eyes wide, lifting her hand then reaching for the phone.

"Where's Ruby?" he asked, racing towards the desk and slamming his palms down on it. "Where's the woman I arrived with?"

Veronica took the phone off its cradle, finger poised over one of the buttons on the keypad. "She left."

"Who with?" he demanded.

"I'm not at liberty to —"

"I don't give a shit that you're not at liberty." He slapped the desk again, his skin stinging. "Who took her?"

"Took her?" Veronica smiled warily, a frown creating two deep lines between her eyes. "She looked happy enough to me when she walked out of here. All I can say is she was with another Dom. I assumed —"

"You assumed wrong. She used to be with an abusive Dom, someone who comes *here*, and I need to know his address."

"I can't give you that information, you know that."

"Look. Veronica. Please."

She shook her head.

"Then I'll call the police and you can tell them," he snapped, searching his pockets for his mobile. "Fuck it!" He leaned over the desk. "Give me that phone." He snatched it from her.

"Shit, you're serious!" Veronica said, standing and wrenching the phone back. She glanced towards the couple on the sofa then sat, tapping at her computer keyboard. "I am so not meant to be doing this, and if you're asked, you didn't get the information from me, right?"

"Whatever, just tell me what I need to know."

She twisted her monitor so it faced him. He read the address and left the club without thanking her, mind full of what that bastard could be doing to Ruby right now, what he could have done during the elapsed time since Harry had seen her last, however long that had been.

In his car, he backed out of the parking lot, knowing he risked an accident on the ice as he swerved out onto the road. His heart thundered and he wanted to throw up, so damn angry that Ruby's former Master had claimed her back. Harry gripped the steering wheel, navigating the roads and cursing every stop light, every person who chose to walk out in front of him, every other driver who occupied the streets.

It took less than ten minutes to reach his destination, but it was too much time as far as he was concerned. He drew to a skidding halt outside the house and leapt out of his car, raced to the front door and smacked the shit out of it with the side of his fist. A shadowy figure appeared on the other side of the opaque glass, and he bunched his hands ready to sock the bastard one.

The door swung open, and Nigel Freeman stared at Harry with a look of incomprehension. "Yes?" He frowned and lifted his chin.

"Where's Ruby?"

"Ruby?" He appeared genuinely perplexed.

"The woman you left the club with. Where is she?"

"Oh, *Margaret!*" He shrugged. "She wanted to be dropped in the city centre. Said something about getting a bagel and coffee in that late-night place that just opened. Why? Is there a problem?"

"Late-night bagel place?" *I'll fucking kill you if you mess me around...* "And where is that?"

Nigel smiled. "Now that I can't tell you."

A tic flickered beneath Harry's eye. "You had better—"

"I can't tell you because I don't know, haven't yet seen it myself, and I wouldn't go there anyway. Bagels aren't my thing. Listen, do you want to come in? I have her mobile number in my phone. I can give it to you. Just because we're not together anymore, doesn't mean I don't wish her well with someone new." He stepped back and held out his arm, an invitation for Harry to go inside. "Assuming she's with you now, that is."

"Yes, she is very much with me now." Harry gave him a warning glare, hating the fact he was stepping inside this man's house, but if it meant finding Ruby, he'd do it.

Nigel didn't seem at all jumpy, like someone would if they'd taken a woman against her will. Maybe he had encountered Ruby after someone else had clocked Harry one on the head and left him in that dungeon. Maybe she'd got away from whoever the hell that was and asked Nigel to give her a lift into the city. But why the hell would she want to go to the bagel shop and have a coffee, for God's sake? Why didn't she ask him to take her to Harry's house instead? Had she just been playing Harry, waiting for the right time to leave him? He thought about whether she'd have her phone with her, whether he'd even seen her *with* one, and came up blank.

Shit!

Grinding his teeth, he followed Nigel from room to room, getting the feeling the man was purposely making out he'd misplaced his phone and couldn't find it. They ended up in the dining room, where Nigel let out a happy "Ah!" and picked up his phone off a sideboard.

"Here it is. Let me just scroll through and get her number. You can punch it into yours as I call it out."

Harry took a deep breath. "I don't have my phone. Please, just write it down."

Nigel *tsked* good-naturedly and led the way back to the front door. He paused at a telephone table and scribbled on a pad, tearing the top sheet off and handing it to Harry. "Would you like to call her from my phone? Although...hmmm, I doubt she'll answer if she sees my number come up. We had a pleasant enough conversation in the car, but she might get the wrong idea and think my seeing her again has given me ideas about getting back together, you understand? No offence, but I'm over her. She's...not my type, I realised that just before we split up."

Harry grimaced. "You split up? When?"

Nigel stared at the ceiling, thinking. "Oh, about a fortnight ago. She left on a Monday morning, bags packed, off into a taxi. Think she said she was going back to her mother's. Would you like her address?"

Harry nodded, mind whirling with this new information. It was looking more and more like Ruby had spun him a line, had well and truly hooked him, used him. He should be angry with her but he was damned if he could be. It didn't matter what she'd told him or why, he'd fallen for her and wanted her back.

The realisation stunned him. He'd never allowed anyone to get away with lying to him, had never known deep in his heart that the lies didn't matter because they always had, yet with Ruby...

Nigel took the paper back and wrote out an address.

"Would you mind if I used your bathroom?" Harry asked.

Nigel looked up from writing. "Of course not! Upstairs, second door on the right."

The man might seem calm and collected, might not be harbouring Ruby, but Harry needed to check upstairs for peace of mind. He followed Nigel's directions, scoping out every room, looking under beds and inside wardrobes.

Nothing.

He went into the bathroom and closed the door, stood there for two minutes, then flushed the toilet. He washed his hands, conscious he was using valuable time, but didn't want Nigel to know what he'd suspected. He returned downstairs to find a smiling Nigel waiting where he'd left him.

"Yes," Nigel said. "I'd try her mother's. I imagine she'll be there by now. I dropped her at the bagel place well over two hours ago."

Two hours? Harry had been out of it in the dungeon for that long? He glanced at his watch just to make sure. Jesus Christ, it was after midnight.

Unable to bring himself to thank Nigel, he nodded curtly and left the house, deciding to check out the bagel shop first instead. Although Nigel had seemed unperturbed by his visit, Harry had a niggling doubt in his mind regarding the man. Surely Ruby couldn't have made up such awful abuse. Her telling of it had been genuine, he was sure of it. Then he winced, knowing full well how people could cuckold you, make you believe they were innocent when they weren't. He prided himself in being able to spot a liar from a mile away — his profession had taught him that — yet there was always a first time in reading someone wrong...

He sped into the city, glad the roads were clear and had been gritted, taking advantage of the free parking after seven p.m. in an out-of-the-way lot. He strode towards a couple canoodling in a pub doorway and called out, "The new bagel place. Where is it?"

The couple broke apart, and the man looked at Harry as though he'd lost his mind.

"Bagel place? Don't know what you're on about, mate."

Harry pulled in a lungful of cold air, blowing it out forcefully in order to calm his raging nerves. "I was told there's a new bagel place, open late."

The man shook his head. "Nope, think someone's pulling your leg."

Harry closed his eyes momentarily then raised a hand in thanks as he stumbled away from them, heading back to his car. The knowledge that Nigel had successfully lied to him sparked such violent anger inside him he had to lean on his bonnet to stop himself throwing up.

"Bastard!" he shouted, lifting his hand then slapping it down. "You fucking, utter bastard!"

He wrenched his car door open and jumped inside, gunning the engine and backing out of his space. He raced back to Nigel's, stopping down the road a little. God, his heart hurt from beating so fast. Pains streaked across his chest, and he pleaded with whichever God would listen that he wouldn't have a panic or heart attack. His whole body filled with energy—foreign energy he'd never experienced before, as though an overload of adrenaline was flooding his system, threatening to take him out.

The thought of Ruby somewhere in there spurred Harry into getting out of the car and walking to stand outside the house, seeing all the lights were off. Where could she be, though? He'd checked everywhere except the garage. Maybe the man had a shed…

He crept onto Nigel's driveway, going to the garage and pressing his ear to one of the door edges. It was silent inside, but that didn't mean a thing. Ruby could be asleep, trussed up, drugged up… His stomach rolled over, and he called her name into the few millimetres of space between the door and metal jamb. Waiting only seconds for a response and receiving none, he took the narrow path down the side of the house and headed for a six-foot wooden gate at the bottom. It opened when he turned the circular iron handle, and he stepped into the rear garden, seeing nothing but trees around the edges and lawn in the centre.

Frustrated and beginning to panic, he moved to the house, sidling along the brick until he came to a window. He peered inside, seeing the darkened kitchen. He went along further, the glow of an interior light splashing onto cream-and-pink patio slabs. Mindful he might be spotted, he pressed his front to the wall beside the window and leaned across enough that only one half of his face could be seen if someone nosed outside.

The dining room didn't look the same as it had when he'd been in there. The table and chairs had been pushed to the side, rug and all, revealing a square hole, a slatted wooden door open and flush to the floor. He frowned, trying to comprehend what he was seeing, realisation coming on so swiftly he had to hold back a howl of rage. The bastard had her in some kind of cellar?

He had the urge to smash the damn window and break in but knew the law too well. He'd be the one at fault if he went inside and found Ruby was there of her own free will. Anxious, and without a phone to call the police, he dithered in indecision long enough to see Ruby's head then body appear out of the hole. She stood beside the dining table, gaze fixed on the square in the floor, her face unreadable. She looked neither happy nor sad, just so damn neutral Harry wasn't sure of the best course of action to take. Should he knock on the window, letting her know he was here? If she saw him, he'd be able to tell from her initial reaction whether she was relieved to see him.

He lifted his hand ready to tap then stopped. Nigel came out of the hole. He closed the door, pulled the rug and furniture back into place, and jammed his hands on his hips. Ruby nodded, looking over Nigel's shoulder, and her eyes widened just enough for Harry to know she'd seen him.

Nigel took her arm and she trailed him across the room. He disappeared through the doorway, and Ruby glanced at the window again.

"*Help me!*" she mouthed.

Harry ran out of the garden and onto the street. He raced up the path of the neighbour living next door and jabbed at the doorbell several times. The chime tinkled inside, over and over until an interior light snapped on. The door opened a crack, a security chain preventing it opening fully, and a woman stared out at him, worry etched on her face.

"Phone!" he said. "I need to use your phone. Next door...the man next door—"

"I don't want anything to do with him. He's weird." The woman made to close the door.

Harry stuck his foot in the gap. "Please! Phone the police. He's abducted my girlfriend!"

Chapter Fifteen

"I wouldn't try anything if I were you," Master said, guiding her out of the dining room. "Like I said, we're going to play."

She held her head high and her shoulders firm. He wouldn't break her no matter what happened now. Harry was here. She'd be safe.

"You think he's going to come and save you, don't you? Not likely." He tugged her up the stairs, heading for the spare room. "You're not worth the time or the effort. You're nothing but a slut who needs a firm hand."

He smacked her arse. When Harry tapped her there it was erotic and turned her on, but this did nothing for her except make bile rise into her throat. This was abuse in its purest form, a spiteful whack intended to hurt, not bring pleasure. Anyway he could hurt her, he would.

Ruby walked along the landing and waited while he opened the door. He pushed her inside. She stumbled forward and turned to face the doorway. Was being in this room just a reprieve? Did he plan on keeping her underground for the most part? What if Harry came in to save her and Nigel did what he'd promised he'd do? She'd be stuck here at his mercy, the love of her life dead.

She shuddered. No, she wouldn't go back down there again. Rubbing her arms, she waited, knowing she'd either get out of this house alive or die trying.

"You know what I'm going to do to you?" Nigel asked.

Ruby nodded and looked past his shoulder. She couldn't bear to see him gloating at his power.

He closed and locked the door, then took her arm and propelled her to the bed where all of his torture equipment was set. He could keep her here for hours if he dealt with Harry. Bound and gagged. No one would be able to hear her scream or even know where she was.

Nigel put the lights on over the bed and started to strip off his shirt. "Take off your clothes," he ordered, going over to the straps on the headboard. Nigel had an assortment of things on that headboard — straps, handcuffs, leather bindings — to keep her contained during his discipline sessions, each one designed to inflict more pain than the last time she'd been held.

Ruby didn't argue or question him. He was way bigger than her and could easily overpower her, making it harder to defend herself later if he broke one of her bones.

She stripped and he beckoned to her. She moved over to him and stood beside the bed, nerves jangling.

Harry, please hurry.

Nigel shoved her onto the bed facedown and took one of her hands and then the other, strapping her wrists to the headboard. He tied her legs to the metal footer. Once she was secure, he stood and turned a wheel attached to the wall. Her hands lifted further and further above her head, her chest and pelvis rising from the mattress, the headboard growing in height until she gasped, stretched too tightly. Pain scoured her muscles and tendons, and she knew she had to tune it out in order to get through this. If she concentrated on the pain it exacerbated it.

In this pose she was useless, unable to fight any of his punishments. She remembered another time on this bed, where he'd whipped her, given her the scars she now carried around with her daily. Before she could feel sorry for herself, she pinned all her hopes on Harry rescuing her.

Hurry, Harry.

Ruby kept looking at the door. It would be only a matter of moments before Nigel laid into her. He hummed as he went to his table of weapons and picked up the paddle, similar to the one Harry had used.

"I've got to break you again in order to mould you. This is all Harry's fault. You shouldn't have left me."

He walked back to her, stroked her cheek, his thumb running along her lower lip. The desire to bite down on him was so strong but she kept it all locked in. It wouldn't do her any good, strapped up as she was. If anything, it would make his punishment worse. Nigel climbed on the bed and straddled her, his arse settling on the backs of her calves. He stuffed rough material into her mouth. She cringed, hung her head and closed her eyes, breathing through her nose, the intake of air not enough. He caressed her back then cupped her naked breasts, moving down to her pussy.

Ruby prayed.

"Such a shame my work has been ruined," he said, taking his hands off her.

Ruby heard the rush of air as the paddle was raised and waited, tension building inside her.

Harry, please, come for me. Save me.

Treacherous tears poured down her face and her heart pounded.

Whack!

The paddle slapped the side of her leg followed by another strike on her arse. These were not small love taps but full-on force. Ruby fought to contain her scream. As the paddle connected with her exposed body for a third time, she released it, ineffectual with her mouth filled the way it was.

Sweat dotted her forehead and the need to be sick came with the burning throb of what he'd done. Nigel kept on. The pain was excruciating. This was worse than any other beatings he'd given her. He now had to prove his manhood, prove she belonged to him. As he paddled harder, Ruby couldn't distinguish the time between slaps anymore. Her body was one giant ball of pain.

In no time at all, she went limp, the swat of the paddle never-ending on her legs and arse. She knew from the force of the impacts she'd be bruised and possibly even bleeding in places.

Harry, please. I can't hold on much longer.

She tried to think of everything to do with Harry to keep her focused. Meeting him. His wonderful sense of humour. His posh exterior hiding the fact that deep down inside he was a true gentleman and a classic Dom. Harry made her want to be better and to make him proud. Her mum would really like him, even with his fancy suits and silly sayings.

God, I love you, Harry.

The kiss in the chip shop was the most memorable, the moment of them passing into a different phase of their relationship. All couples had them, a turning point or a crossroads. Harry and his kiss had changed her.

I love you, Harry.

If nothing else ever came of their time together, she knew in her heart of hearts she would always love that man.

The pain grew unbearable. She couldn't fight it anymore.

Ruby closed her eyes. She prayed for the sweet relief of darkness, while accompanied by the macabre sounds of Nigel's heaving breaths and wretched snarls as he used all his might to paddle her into complete submission.

* * * *

Harry stood on the path outside Nigel's house, the woman beside him bundled up in a coat over her pink fleece dressing gown. She'd called the police, handing him the phone through the door crack when he'd shouted to ask her to let him speak. Once she realised he wasn't some crazy bastard out to trick his way into her home, she'd unlatched the chain and allowed him to finish the call in her living room. He paced as he spoke, itched to go next door and break in, but something told him not to. The lawyer in him battled for prominence over his natural male instinct and won. If anything happened to Ruby because of that he'd never forgive himself.

He stared up the street, longing for sight of a police car.

What kind of man am I, waiting out here like this?

Shoving what he 'should' do aside, he gave in and went with what he wanted to do. He ran towards Nigel's front door and hammered on it with the side of his fist, yelling that he'd kill the bastard if he did anything to hurt Ruby. He expected lights to come on, for Nigel to open the door and act as though nothing untoward was going on inside, but the house remained in darkness. Frustrated, he rushed around the back. The dining room light was still on. He glanced up and saw light bleeding around the edges of an upper window, curtains drawn against any neighbours in the houses behind who might see what was happening inside. Knowing it was undoubtedly a bedroom, he cursed, thinking of what Ruby had told him about the torture devices Nigel had used on her in the past.

"Fuck doing the right thing," he said, streaking to the back door and yanking at the handle.

He raised his arm ready to punch the glass, but a shuffle of footsteps had him holding his fist mid-air. He turned and saw the woman neighbour peering at him around the corner of the house.

"What are you doing?" she said, voice full of urgency. "The police are here!"

He brushed past her, running out to the front. Two officers in uniform stood on Nigel's doorstep, one peering through the letterbox, the other tapping with the brass knocker. They stared at him as though he was the man they were after.

"You have to get in there. He's got her. Took her —"

"Now hang on a moment, sir." The officer who'd been looking through the letterbox straightened, holding out one hand as if to ward Harry off. "We don't know that anything is actually going on here.

Yes, you called it in, but we have to knock before taking the next course of action."

"Knock harder then!" he roared at the other policeman. "I'm telling you, I saw him bring her up out of a door in the floor. Go around the back and look if you don't believe me, but bloody hell, get a damn move on. He's a sadistic bastard, could be doing anything to her in there." He clenched his hands into fists, wanting to shoulder barge the door and find Ruby himself.

Red tape pissed him the hell off and brought a redder mist down over his eyes.

"Calm down, sir —"

"Calm down? Fucking calm down? Jesus Christ!" He strode to the door and pushed the officer aside. "Have me up for breaking and entering for all I care. I'm going in, something I should have done ages ago!"

The officer gripped his shoulders and pulled him back. Harry resisted, straining forward, hoping the officer's hold would break.

It didn't.

A light coming on in Nigel's hallway stopped any further tussle. Harry straightened up, hating the policeman's hands still being on his shoulders. The door opened, and Nigel, fully dressed in a suit of all things, stood in the threshold.

"Can I help you?" he asked, as calm as he'd been when Harry had been here earlier.

"It's him," Harry said, renewing his attempt to make the officer let him go. "He's got her in there!"

Nigel cocked his head. "What on earth is this man talking about?" He looked at the policemen, his expression one belonging to a bemused man.

"Let them in if you've got nothing to hide!" Harry shouted, shrugging and failing to get the policeman off him. It ignited more anger inside him, but if he struck a man of the law he'd find himself in shit. "I know you have her in there."

"Who are you talking about?" Nigel asked, frowning.

"You know exactly who I mean. Ruby!"

"Ruby? I don't know a Ruby." He smiled, the condescending bastard, and held one hand out inside his home. "Please, *officers*, feel free to take a look around. You won't find anyone else in here but me."

Nigel stepped back. Harry gathered all his strength and lunged forward, freeing himself. He shoved Nigel in the chest and entered his house, ignoring the shouts behind him — Nigel blustering about Harry being clearly insane, the officers shouting he had no right to be inside.

Harry fled up the stairs, working out which room the light had come from. His heart pounded so hard he found it difficult to breathe, but he pressed on, surging down the hallway to the only door that light filtered beneath. He gripped the handle and turned it, but the door had been locked. Muffled grunts came from the other side, spurring him into smacking his side against the door repeatedly. Pain lashed at him, streaking through his shoulder and down his back, and he gritted his teeth as he bashed at the door again. He was aware of heavy footsteps on the stairs and Nigel still swearing innocence, and then the door gave. He staggered inside, eyes widening at the horrific sight before him.

Ruby was strapped to a bed, her arms, legs and torso stretched to unquestionably painful levels. Red welts marred her back, arse and thighs, the harsh light above her highlighting trickles of translucent fluid and blood from the wounds. He ran to the side of the bed, leaning over to pull the hair back from her face, to check she was still breathing. She lifted her head and turned it so she faced him. Tears streaked her cheeks, her lashes soaked with them, and her lips stretched around a wad of bunched-up white cloth in her mouth. He snatched it out and she gasped for air, at the same time trying to speak but failing to get any words out.

"Don't speak," he said. "Just breathe. I'm here. The police are here."

He took his gaze off her and looked at the headboard. The straps that bound her were leather, the silver buckles large. He lost no time in undoing one, managing to give her some relief before one of the policemen burst into the room.

"Jesus Christ!" he said, going back out into the hallway. "Secure him!" he shouted, then moved to the other side of the bed to tackle the other wrist buckle.

"Oh, God!" Ruby croaked. "Don't let him see me like this. Please, don't…"

"Shh," Harry said, releasing one ankle. "It's okay. You're safe now. No one's ever going to hurt you again, understand?"

She nodded, her torso lowering to the bed, and he lay beside her, gathering her into his arms. The policeman untied her other ankle and stood in the doorway, speaking into his radio.

Everything faded away — everything except Harry and Ruby. He kissed the top of her head, squeezing her to him, conscious of his sleeve brushing her back and likely causing her more pain. His eyes prickled with emotion at the way she clung to him so tightly. She sobbed, her tears wetting his chest, and he resisted stroking her back to comfort her. The welts were angry, raw, and the sight of them made him feel sick.

If he wasn't involved in this mess he'd have gladly taken Ruby's case and fought tooth and nail to ensure Nigel was put behind bars, but he couldn't do it, wouldn't be allowed to.

No, but I know a man who can.

* * * *

His hallway wall was cold against Master's cheek at first, but it soon warmed. One of the policemen had cuffed his hands at his lower back and now stood behind him, splayed hand on Master's head, pinning him in place.

Master sighed. He really hadn't wanted this to happen. It had the potential to be a mess, but he'd soon straighten it out. He'd play the BDSM card, where he made them see no one in the lifestyle understood the rules, how it appeared to the casual onlooker that he had been abusing Margaret, but that wasn't the case. No, she was his sub and he had every right to treat her this way—especially because she hadn't said no, hadn't said a safe word. She wouldn't be able to deny it, and if he could get to see her before he was taken to the police station, he'd give her a look that left her in no doubt that if she told the police lies he'd have Harry seen to.

It didn't turn out that way. Two more officers arrived, burlier than the others, taking him away in the back of their car, neither of them speaking. That was all right. He'd explain once they began interviewing him, would get character witnesses to let them know this had all been a silly mistake. That Harry wanted Margaret for himself and would do anything, including this, to have her.

Yes, that will work.

The lights of the oncoming city grew in number as the car took Nigel to the place where everything would be smoothed over. He hummed, the same tune that he'd filled the room with as he'd trussed Margaret up. He wondered whether she'd shiver with revulsion every time she heard it in the future, whether she'd carry her hate for him inside her for the rest of her life.

He hoped so.

His cock hardened at the thought of *that*.

At the sight of the police station, Master quietly sucked in a breath. He had never been inside one, had never planned to be either, but if things went how he envisaged, he wouldn't be in this one for very long. He smiled as the car drew to a halt around the back, smiled as the officers led him into the building, and smiled some more when he was guided into an interview room and asked to take a seat.

He sat and waited, with a different officer standing beside the door, and ran through his story in his mind. He had no doubt they'd find the underground room, but that was all right. There was nothing in it, and he wondered what he should tell him he was going to use it for.

A private club. Yes, that would do it. A place where he could entertain his friends. He allowed his thoughts to meander down that route, nodding as he thought of the bare plaster, ready, he would tell them, for the soundproofing men to come in. After all, if he was going to throw parties, he wouldn't want the beat of music to upset his neighbours. No, he was a good citizen, only wishing to be left alone in peace to live his life.

Margaret would be a good girl, he was sure of it. She'd tell them Harry had no business ringing the police like that. After all, if things went wrong and he *was* convicted—it wouldn't come to that…of course it wouldn't—he'd be out in short time, wouldn't he?

Surely she wouldn't run the risk of him coming back to find her.

Chapter Sixteen

Four Years Later

Ruby stood in the living room, looking out at the frozen ground. Christmas was a few weeks away, but she wasn't looking at the snow with Christmas in mind or for the season of goodwill. She was looking at the place where four years ago her life had changed forever.

If Harry hadn't come out that night to find her, she wouldn't have lasted much longer with that bastard Nigel, who was now rotting in some prison miles away.

She went into the kitchen and washed the last of the dishes, placing them on the drainer. Peeling off her rubber gloves, she gazed at the diamond ring circling her finger. A few months after that fateful night, Harry had proposed and given her a whirlwind engagement and an even bigger pre-wedding present — she finally had her name changed to something she would want to hear. She couldn't imagine being a Margaret anymore, and so before their wedding she legally changed her name to Ruby. He'd also gifted her with a collar, a diamond choker to save people looking at her oddly and asking questions—a collar she could wear all the time.

He'd explained about the mirrors, too. When teaching, he'd wanted his subs to love themselves, to be able to see their bodies and faces often without fretting on how they looked—to learn to accept themselves as they were...beautiful, as he saw them. There was no need for the mirrors now he'd given up teaching other women, and Ruby had started loving herself from the day she'd met Harry, but they remained in place—they made for good sex. Watching them together was a huge turn-on for her.

"What have I told you, Ruby?"

Harry's voice broke across her thoughts, sending a shiver of delight through her body. Smiling, she turned until she butted against the sink, her naked breasts thrust up, cream gathering between her legs. Harry, with his words, had the ability to take her from frozen to molten heat within seconds.

"Why, Sir, I was simply doing the pots."

How she loved this game. Harry would give her an order—a simple order of don't do anything—and she'd do something, anything, just to push him a little over the edge. Her punishment would be severe indeed.

"I told you to wait here, in this chair and not to move."

Harry held onto the back of the pine chair she usually sat in, and Ruby imagined the time last week when he had sat in the very same chair and demanded she ride him to completion. Many times he put her in charge of their lovemaking and tested her in new, delicious ways.

"I guess I couldn't help myself," she said softly, bowing her head into her submissive pose.

Nothing would ever rush Harry. He moved slowly until he stood in front of her. Ruby stared at the floor, hoping to keep the smile off her face. So many times before she'd allowed her humour to interfere with their play.

Placing a finger under her chin, he tilted her head back and, as always, he took her breath away. A true Master in every way. Disappointment clouded his face, but the underlying affection he had for her began shining through.

Harry never covered or hid his true feelings from her. She knew and would always know he loved her completely.

"I think my little Ruby needs a spank."

Like all the times before, she bit her lip and contained the moan threatening to release. Having his hands on her would be a pleasure to behold. He knew how to tease her to the very limits, topple her over the edge and catch her, joining her in the abyss of sensation.

"Yes, Sir, I've been very naughty," she encouraged.

"Hmm. I think you like my punishments a little too much. Maybe I should leave you to deal with your lack of discipline on your own."

Harry made to turn and Ruby panicked. A few weeks ago she'd given herself to him along with her ability to self-pleasure. He was in complete control and could bring or take pleasure from her.

"No, Sir, please, I need your punishment." She immediately went to her knees in front of him, bringing her face directly level with his cock.

The large shaft was outlined in his trousers, showing her effect on him.

They paused with him standing over her and Ruby on her knees—a pose she knew drove him to distraction. A test of wills.

He ran his fingers through her hair and she knew he'd give in. This was the idea of their play, to show her that even with him as Master she still had the ability to work a scene. His sub would always have a say in what happened.

"I think you've tested me too much." He sighed.

Her heart kicked a beat. God, she loved this man with her whole being.

He moved to sit in the chair she'd thought about earlier. He sat and patted his knee. Without thought, she followed his instruction, standing in front of him, turning round so he could see the full arse she had now. Ready and waiting to be spanked. She perched on his knee, not wanting to hurt him. She'd put a few pounds on since being with him. No longer did her bones protrude but each curve was nicely rounded and gave him something to hold onto without fear of breaking her.

He cupped her waist and brought her back against his chest, moving his fingers down her body in a slow, agonising caress.

"You're shuddering. Tell me, sweet Ruby, do you want release?"

"Yes, Master, always."

She gasped as his fingers brushed over her mound, enough to send waves of sensation through her body but not enough to start her on the main road to pleasure.

Releasing a moan of frustration, he moved down past her cunt to caress her legs. He grasped them, opened them wider.

"I wish I had a mirror so I could see how wet you are. To see this pretty pussy. Who owns this pussy?"

"You do."

"You do, what?"

"You do...Master."

She groaned as his finger ran through her wet heat, dripping just from the simple touch.

"Have you been playing with yourself?" he asked.

"No!" she cried in denial.

"No, what?"

"No, Master, I'd never play with myself without your permission. It is forbidden, Master."

His cock thrust up against her leg at her words.

"Should I punish you?"

"I will accept everything Master has to offer."

He pushed a finger inside her, his action easy from how wet she was just from being near him. She cried out. Her clit felt like it was ready to explode, and he purposefully didn't touch it.

"Please, Master..." She flung her head back and closed her eyes, biting her lips together to keep another cry from rushing out. She wanted to order him to touch her but she knew how much worse her punishment would be. He'd make sure her pleasure lasted until the last possible moment instead of giving it to her straightaway.

"Are you telling me what to do, Ruby?"

"No, Master."

He took his hands away. She whimpered at the loss.

"I think you need a spank, sub. To have this rounded arse hot and red."

Her pussy gushed more cream. His punishments always had the ability to make her crave the forbidden.

"Over my knee," he ordered, gently pushing her off his lap to the floor.

Within seconds, she leaned over his knees, her arse in the air ready for punishment. She panted and juices leaked onto the tops of her inner thighs.

Spank me, Harry. Make it burn.

Throughout the years, Harry had managed to master the art of seduction with her, and she knew deep in her heart Harry Knowles was the right man for her. In the society world he was a man to be respected and his rules adhered to—the same as in their private life—but more than that, in the comfort of their home he was the man she could and would love for the rest of her life. He'd never, in all their time together, left her feeling frightened.

"Look at this arse. I could stare at it all night long."

His hands roamed the cheeks, fingers biting as he squeezed. She moaned and thrust up to meet him, wanting everything he had to offer.

One hand stilled and he slid the other up her back, moving her hair out of the way. Harry always did this to her. Touched her, warming her up ready to receive her punishments. Afterwards, she couldn't form a coherent thought let alone refuse the man she loved.

Smack!

The first hit shocked her even though she knew it was coming. She gasped and held onto the length of his trouser leg. Exhaling, she enjoyed the heated sting followed by the cool air as he blew over the site. She imagined his hand print clear on her white flesh. He demanded she did not expose her arse to the sun. He liked it pale—easier for him to see his marks.

"Lovely."

Smack, smack, smack.

The sound echoed round the room, her arse stinging. He delved his fingers into the heat of her cunt. She cried out, wondering if there would be a wet patch on his trousers when he was done.

"You're dripping," he said.

"I know," Ruby said, not thinking, forgetting to add 'Master'.

He landed another three harsh swipes to her arse. She whimpered and ground her pussy lips onto his leg. The sensation was too much. She needed release before she lost her mind.

Harry picked her up and carried her up the stairs. Ruby held on to him, trusting him in everything. In no time at all he had her in the middle of their bed, making her wait while he took off his clothes. She loved watching him undress, the surprise body underneath his prim and proper suits always a delightful distraction.

"You like what you see, sub?"

"Always."

"Good. Arms above your head and legs out."

Ruby didn't think to argue and did as he asked straightaway. He tied her hands to the headboard then her feet to the footer, careful to make sure she wasn't tied too tightly.

"Are they good?"

"Yes, Master."

Only when he was certain of that would he join her on the bed. Ruby watched him, her heart beating rapidly as she spied the lighted candle he'd brought with him.

"Where did that come from?" she asked.

He quirked a brow at her lack of formal address. "I have my ways. Just like I have this."

He lifted a bottle of water, and Ruby frowned, wondering what on earth he'd need it for. He opened the bottle and in a steady drop, chilled water landed on her breasts. Never before had Ruby felt anything like it. She arched up as the cold engulfed her tight nipple, followed immediately by the drop of warm candle wax.

Ruby screamed in pleasure, and Harry continued tormenting her, alternating the cold with bursts of heat along her body.

After a while of teasing her body to fresh heights, he still refused to fuck her and give her the release she sought. Harry disappeared off to the bathroom, coming back with a cloth and a small basin of water. He cleaned the water and the wax from her body.

"Please, Master…"

"Not Master. Harry."

He did that every now and again. When he tried something new like the candle he'd demand she call him by his given name, almost as if making sure she knew who he really was.

"Did you like?"

"I love everything you do to me. I trust you, Master."

"I love you."

Harry moved the water and cloth, then leant down to kiss her. Still bound as she was, she let him take control of the kiss, moaning when his tongue thrust deep, melding with her own. His lips were a wicked turn-on.

Ruby smiled. He eased down her body, her legs already splayed open for him to do whatever he wanted. Harry got on the bed between her legs. She held her breath, waiting, her pussy burning with the need to have him touch her in any way he was willing. The flesh heated under his gaze, her cream dribbling down to her arse crack. She closed her eyes, waiting, waiting. He swiped his tongue through her slit, feasting on her. She panted, holding back screams of delight, thrashing against the restraints in mock protest. She wanted to hold his head and push herself against his face.

"Please, please..." She gasped, not knowing what she begged for.

With her climax fast approaching and the delicious build of completion starting, Harry moved up her body, his chin glistening with her spent juice.

"Why did you stop?" she whimpered, still without a climax, her body crying out for one.

He shoved his cock inside her all the way to the hilt. Pulling on the restraints, she groaned, stuttered sounds that hurt her throat.

"Fuck, so tight and hot, Ruby."

Harry cupped her face and stared into her eyes, pulling all the way out before plunging back inside. She kept her gaze on his eyes, the connection somehow deeper than the intimacy they shared. He pushed in as far as he could but still his gaze remained on her.

His body calling her to pleasure was nothing compared to the love shining out of his eyes. Ruby thought she could see his very heart and soul. The ultimate understanding and vital chemistry between two people. Far more powerful than the hormones releasing in her, their love alive and pulsing between them.

"I love you," she gasped out.

His eyes dilated. "You're my very life."

He pummelled his cock inside her and she welcomed the sweet release he could give. He slid one hand between her legs and flicked her swollen clit.

"Come for me, baby."

His command took her over the edge. She pulled on her wrist restraints, wanting to hold him, to grab him and claw at him. Instead, she gripped him with her thighs as she rode the wave of bliss.

"Fuck, yeah, come all over my cock. Fuck, your cunt is fucking tight," he said, his language, as always, going downhill as his climax neared.

Ruby loved hearing his hoarse voice, the erotic sounds teasing her.

He fucked her faster, driving harder.

She knew he wouldn't last. With one final thrust, he slammed his lips down on hers and kissed her, pushing his tongue deep. He tensed his body, and she tasted her juices from his tongue at the same time as feeling the kick of his cock as his release shot out. Ruby came with him, shuddering and bucking, pressing her clit against him for double the ecstasy.

He collapsed on top of her, breathing ragged, his thundering heartbeat pulsing on her chest. She waited for him to catch his breath, to come down before lightly tugging on her bonds for him to release hers. The moment she was free, she hugged him to her.

"I love you," he growled, his head resting on her breast.

"Do you love me or your cushions?"

He playfully bit the side of her breast, laughing. "I love these." He lifted his head and held them, rubbing his face in the mounds.

Ruby giggled. "Mr Harry Knowles, rubbing his face in a woman's tits. What would people say?"

"The same as what they would at me marrying a woman who is apparently beneath me but I love her completely." He kissed her, then pulled away to stare down at her.

"My mother expected nothing less than you making a respectable woman out of me."

"If she could see you now... There's nothing respectable about you."

"Hey!" She swiped at him.

"You know I love you." Harry hugged her to him, chuckling.

"Speaking of my mother, she's coming for Christmas providing we can get out in the snow to collect her."

"We've just made love and you want to talk about your mother?" he teased.

"Some men go straight to sleep, but I find you're a lot more willing to agree when I ask after you've been laid."

"Only because you're naked and I can get what I want again afterwards."

He nibbled her breast and Ruby sighed in contentment.

One of the things she loved about him was, soon after finding her that night at Nigel's, he'd taken her to go and see her mother. The reunion had been emotional, full of tears and hugs. Ruby hadn't known Nigel had threatened her mother with the loss of her house and even her life if she got in touch with her only daughter. Hearing of the threats from the man who'd destroyed her life up until she'd met Harry broke her heart but, as always, he'd been there to catch her, hold her when she thought she couldn't cope with the new information.

From that day, Mrs Savage had demanded Harry care for Ruby completely. Not that Ruby needed her mother's demands made on her behalf. Nigel was well and truly put away, probably someone's bitch on the inside. Harry and her mother had talked for hours while Ruby sat and drank tea, watching them both interact and loving the sense of a complete family at last.

"I love your mother," Harry said, pulling her from her thoughts. "But I don't want to think about her while I'm in bed with my wife. That said, I'll do what I can to get her up here for you."

He splayed a hand over her stomach. She knew what he was thinking. They had decided to try for a baby, but the past few months had been unsuccessful. They wanted the special news in time to give to her mother for Christmas, but Ruby knew that if by the end of the year she hadn't conceived they would go and get tests.

"Do you think you could be?" he asked.

"I don't know. Would it be bad if I wasn't?"

"Of course not, but with you barefoot and pregnant I can guarantee you'll stay with me."

Ruby swiped him again and settled her head more comfortably in the pillows.

"You know while you have money I'll stay," she said, teasing and playing up the role some people had said she'd occupied since the day Harry found her — that of a gold digger.

"I'd believe that if you used the money I gave you."

She accepted his gifts, but she also had a part-time job at the local library and earned her own money. Refusing anything other than gifts had become a long-standing joke, especially when people liked to comment on her lack of family money. Some acquaintances of Harry's really were cynical.

Harry knew her and that was all that mattered.

"I love you, Harry," she whispered, kissing his cheek.

"I know you do, baby."

He held her and Ruby felt safe and comforted by his presence. Whatever the future held she was ready to deal. Four years with Harry had been the best years of her life so far. They'd both had such a rude awakening on life and how people behaved towards them, how people treated them, but she wouldn't change a thing. She smiled at how hers had been literally rude — waking in front of his fire and finding herself embroiled in a hot love affair that turned into something so permanent. She'd long accepted that not everyone was as kind as Harry, who took her at face value and knew she wasn't with him for his money or the standing in society he gave her. She loved her peaceful life of working in the library and returning home to him, where they took it in turns to cook. Loved every damn minute of being a wife and sub. The meals out, holidays, jewels, the shopping trips to buy clothes, bags and shoes — she didn't want any part of it.

She didn't need anything other than his love.

About the Authors

Natalie Dae

Natalie Dae is a multi-published author in three pen names writing several genres. She lives with her husband, children, and three cats in an English village. She writes full time and is also a cover artist and blog designer. In another life she was an editor. Her other pen names are Sarah Masters and Charley Oweson.

Sam Crescent

Sam Crescent has always had a love of fiction, through her teen years she would find friendship between the pages rather than in an actual person. By the time she turned sixteen she discovered mills and boon and never looked back. She loved the quick happily-ever-after read. A guarantee that no matter what happened the heroes and heroines would always find their soul mate. After college and starting a degree, one lonely bored night she searched the internet looking for a new author to read. On that night and for the years to come she discovered romantica and erotic writing.

Natalie Dae and Sam Crescent love to hear from readers. You can find their contact information, website details and author profile page at http://www.total-e-bound.com.

Total-E-Bound Publishing

www.total-e-bound.com

Take a look at our exciting range of literagasmic™
erotic romance titles and discover pure quality
at Total-E-Bound.